BROKEN TRUST

Kristen Cosey

To Letani,
Thank you for your
support! "Never stop following
your dreams!
:)
- Krissy the Author

ISBN: 978-0-578-57410-3

DEDICATION

To my children, Terrence and Malia, I love you. Always follow your
dreams and never let anyone discourage you. Anything you choose to
do; I will always be cheering you on; your #1 fan.
Reach for the stars.

In loving memory of 'Grandma Ruth.' I did it.

BROKEN TRUST

CONTENTS

BROKEN TRUST

ACKNOWLEDGMENTS

Thank you to everyone who believed in me and pushed me to follow my dreams. Thank you for the overwhelming support in helping me release my very first novel. I hope you guys enjoy it.

BROKEN TRUST

PROLOGUE

July

Falling onto the bed, heaving, I felt winded. I heard faint sounds of Minnie scuffling with my dad as I clutched my chest, over my gasping breath. I struggled to get up, to regain my composure.

What did I do to get punched in the chest? I thought. My dad pushed Minnie and she fell back onto the bed, narrowly missing me. It was a hot summer night in July of 2011. The tension in our house was thick like the humidity outside.

"Darnell leave them alone, they didn't do anything" my mom quavered in a low whisper.

I knew she wasn't going to say too much after that, or he would go upside her head as well. In between my blurred vision, I watched my dad's tall and stocky, six-foot frame, disappear out of the room - a bottle of Gin in his hand, with my mother trailed behind him. The scent of strong alcohol lingered as if he were still hovering in the room; it was sickening.

"Are you okay?" Minnie asked concerned.

Minnie was my older sister. We shared a mom but had different dads.

"I'm okay" I whispered.

I wasn't in the mood for talking. I felt like the wind had been knocked out of me.

"He's a fucking bitch, I bet you he wouldn't pull that shit with no real niggas on da' block in Chicago! I hate him!" Minnie boasted.

She was pissed, she was pacing the floor back and forth, pounding her fist.

"We have to get mommy out of here before he really hurts her. I don't know why she chose to leave everything we had in Chicago and move here to Dallas. We had it good. She should've stayed with Marvin, nothing was wrong with him, I liked him."

Marvin was our mom's ex – boyfriend that she had been with for two years right before she was back with my dad.

I was sixteen and Minnie was twenty. Besides Marvin, I didn't recall my mom being with anyone else. My mom hadn't been with Minnie's dad since she was about three years old. That was before I was born or even thought of being conceived.

Minnie was wilder than me and didn't have a problem fighting anyone, no matter how old or big you were. Standing at only five feet tall and weighing only 110 pounds, Minnie was easily challenged until people saw her fight. Minnie was dark-skinned, short with a coke-bottle shape. She also had long curly hair that reached the middle of her back and big lips. She always caught the boy's attention in our neighborhood. I secretly wished I looked like her and was braver like her. She claimed the attention of everyone once she walked in the room. Minnie had the heart of a lion and acted as if she had the strength of a bear. I had seen Minnie defeat so many females & even niggas twice her size. It was just us.

Although our mom never had a son, sometimes I wish we had an older brother that could protect all of us. Who was gonna' protect Minnie if she was always protecting my mom and I? I kept replaying the hit over and over in my head. I was beginning to see my dad in a different light. I tilted my head towards the ceiling desperately trying to stop the tears from escaping, "He's my dad and I'm really starting not to like him, I feel like I don't even know him anymore."

Growing up, I always adored my dad. He could do no wrong in my eyes. This was my first time ever living with him for more than a few months. By the time I had entered the world, my mom and dad were no longer a couple. They reignited their relationship briefly when I was seven but that quickly died after about six months. I had always known the "weekend and holiday" dad. He was the fun dad. I didn't know too much about my dad except what my family would tell me.

About a year ago, my dad proclaimed his love for my mother and asked her to marry him. The news had shocked everyone but who doesn't want to see their parents together and happy? I knew he was one of the biggest hustlas' in Chicago back in the day. He dabbled in a bit of everything. From selling drugs, selling cars, to opening one of the hottest strip clubs in downtown Chicago; he did it all. He ran the hood where we were from. Back then, we had it made. He was older now and wanted a better life than the streets. Even now people thought we had it better than most. We were still always showered with gifts and the finer things, to the world that was enough. All those things came with a price to pay. Behind closed doors, we were living with a monster. No amount of gifts or money could make me happy or content with that. See, I learned at a young age, everything that looked good wasn't good for you.

Minnie wrapped her arms around me which succeeded in making the tears flow.

"It's gone be okay, I'm gone get all of us out of here" she affirmed.

We stayed in the room venting for the remainder of the night. Minnie worked at the local grocery store up the block from our house. She was lucky enough to escape the chaos most of the day. Minnie tried to be as quiet as possible, but it wasn't a big deal because my dad wasn't waking up anytime soon. It became normal for him to come in the house drunk and falling over. He would come in demanding that my mom be a "good wife" and serve him dinner, satisfy his sexual needs, and cough up majority of her money because he claimed he was the "head of the household."

Out of that same mouth, he would say he loves all of us so much, then turn around and call my mom a lazy bitch because she didn't clean something correctly or she was a ho', to show he didn't need her and my mom needed him. Most nights he put on this show when his friends would come over. He made me sick. It was the same nonsense every night. Every time he came home, Minnie and I would retreat to our room until he was knocked out cold drunk.

The worst nights were when he would come home and make himself seem like he was superior to everyone. We were like peasants living in his home. We were forced to eat when he said eat, even my mother. He was our dictator and there was nothing we could do about it unless we were lucky enough to have a reason to get out of the house.

The next few months were hell. My dad was no longer my Superhero, the person I ran to when I was in trouble. He was now the person I ran from. Growing up, I didn't spend much time with him. The times I did spend with my dad were short and obviously misleading of his true character. Shortly after my dad hit me, he became more aggressive with each passing day.

One night, my dad called my sister a hoe. He said she was

only good enough for a good time and that was it. My sister snapped; she was always more vocal than I was. I never wanted to draw attention to myself or say anything back, especially with my dad. My dad jumped in her face and my sister wasn't backing down. She kept hollering; I could tell she was getting under his skin. He was drunk, he tried to grab her, and my sister smacked his hand down.

"Everyone else in this house might be afraid of you but I'm not!" Minnie seethed.

I could feel my heart beating faster. Sweat pooled at my temple and began trickling down my cheek, I was so nervous. I prepared to have to jump in and help my sister.

"Minnie just walk away, please just walk away" my mom begged. My mom was pleading with Minnie, but she wasn't budging. My dad flung Minnie on the couch and Minnie started swinging. I immediately jumped up and tried to pry my dad's hands from Minnie's body.

"Let her go, please, let her go!" My mom pleaded with my dad.

My dad finally let go of Minnie. I quickly grabbed Minnie and held on to her arm,

"Minnie come on, let's go outside" I urged.

"No, I ain't scared of him. He's a bitch ass nigga, I don't ever see him pull this shit on somebody his size!" Minnie shouted.

In the blink of an eye, my dad rushed over and pushed

Minnie so hard that I ended up falling. Minnie stumbled, but she kept her composure.

"Bitch, what the fuck you gone do? You a hood rat, always running the streets" my dad snarled.

I was trying to stay as close as possible to my sister because I wanted to be able to get out of the house with her. I wanted so badly to be back in Chicago with my sister and mom. I never had to worry about my dad because he was never around. I would only hear from him around holidays and expected to meet him at the door with a box of gifts for birthdays and holidays. Everything would be normal again.

Minnie and I managed to get out of the house. Minnie didn't go without a fight, but I slowly pulled her towards the door to make her leave. My mom pleaded with my dad to leave Minnie alone while I kept pulling Minnie towards the door. I feared if I didn't leave with Minnie my dad would lock me in the room for the night.

After weeks of drunken arguments and attacks on Minnie from my dad, she couldn't take it anymore. She got her first and last paycheck from Walmart, where she worked for about three weeks, and left the state. She left for work as normal one day but never returned. A few days later, she called my mom from an anonymous number and told her she was in Atlanta. I hardly ever spoke to

Minnie after that. I missed her but I was also angry. It was just me and my mom going through the scary nights of my drunken father. It was up to me to help my mom fight back when he came home in a drunken state smashing my mom's face into the wall or constantly telling her she's unworthy of anyone better and no one would want her. I was the youngest, I thought everyone was supposed to protect me. My mom and I became pros at packing clothes within two minutes, sleeping in the car, and taking baths in Walmart bathrooms. That was our "go to" place whenever my dad was having one of his drunk episodes. Some nights we were lucky enough to stay at the Hilton hotel when they had nightly specials.

My mom and I endured abuse for about another two years before I decided I'd had enough.

Wham! I jumped off my bed and ran into the living room to see my father scuffling with my mother. I noticed the dining room table knocked over and the family picture on the wall had fallen on the floor; shattered in hundreds of pieces. My dad slammed my mom and pinned her against the wall. I couldn't believe my eyes. My mom was trying so hard to talk.

"Ja-Jas-Jasmine call the police!" She stammered.

My mom tried her best to regulate her breathing, taking long deep breathes while she used her hands to try to protect her stomach. My mom was six months pregnant with twin girls. I was starting to believe my mom couldn't make any boys.

"Go to the neigh-neighbor's house and ca--call the po--police!"

She could barely get the words out, but I didn't need her to. I was out the door, across the yard, and banging on my neighbor's door within thirty seconds.

I banged on the door a few times then waited. The blinds moved so I knew they were home. Besides, they barely went places anyway, they were almost always home, especially at night.

"Please! Can you please call the police? I'm just trying to save my mom. Help us please!" I begged.

I kept banging on the door but all I got in return was dead silence. I hated that my neighbors turned a blind eye to the constant abuse we endured. I knew they heard the constant fights and beatings throughout the night.

So much for doing a good deed and helping someone, I thought.

I ran back in my house and got in my dad's face.

"They're calling the police! You better leave before they show up!" I lied.

I knew my dad didn't want to go back to jail, that was the only way to get him to leave.

"Fuck you bitches!" he bellowed.

"You ain't gone be good for nothing but laying on yo' back just like ya' sister" he bellowed as he shifted his anger towards me.

My dad picked up his wallet off the table and was out the door within the next minute.

9

"Jasmine call the ambulance for me" my mom whimpered holding her head."

"Okay, what's wrong? Is your stomach hurting? What happened to your ear?" I asked.

She was bent over, her chest was heaving in and out profoundly, holding her ear. I fished my mom's cellphone out of her purse, called an ambulance and turned my attention back to her.

"Mom what happened? Why are you holding the side of your face? Did he hit you there?" I asked.

"He didn't really hit me, he just forcefully shoved me by pushing my face." She staggered.

I hated when she tried to downplay anything he did. My mom went to the hospital that night to be monitored just in case something was wrong with the babies.

CHAPTER ONE

Runaway

February

The night I left to go back to Chicago, I went to bed at nine o'clock pretending I was tired. I laid in my bed in the dark until eleven PM, I couldn't miss my bus. The greyhound was scheduled to leave at 1:15 AM. I was determined to leave and never come back. Eleven o' clock rolled around, and I was ready to go. I just needed to get my heavy suitcase out of my small window and climb down from the second floor. I tried to pack light, but it was difficult since I didn't plan on ever coming back. I tried to pack everything that had a special meaning to me.

My sister must have heard the noise because she walked in just as I was pushing my suitcase out of the window. My heart began racing. I hadn't told anyone I was leaving. I was afraid my sister would tell my parents. Sometimes she could hold a secret, but she would sell me out if it benefited her. If this plan didn't work, I would be doomed. "Jasmine where are you going?" Minnie asked. Minnie came back to live with us a year ago after her being shot in the chest during a drive-by shooting in East Atlanta. She figured she could survive occasional fights with my dad than someone constantly trying to shoot at her. "I'm leaving, I'm going back to Chicago. I can't stay here and endure any more beatings from him" I grunted as I struggled to get my suitcase out the windows. *It was my turn to be selfish and think about myself,* I thought.

Minnie didn't say anything else. She immediately began helping me push the suitcase out. I was relieved. "Hurry up! I think they might have heard all the noise" I stressed. I was determined to get out of this house tonight. I was shaking as I tried to get my suitcase outside. My sister, Minnie, and I kept pushing as hard as we could. I was so scared I began crying. Scared my dad would come barging in and beat me to a pulp. Scared I would have to live under the same roof as my father another day. Scared my father would strip all my clothes away from me again and leave me with nothing. Scared.

After one final shove the suitcase landed outside with a thud. I turned to my sister and hugged her. Stepping on the bed, I put one leg out the window followed by the other with my purse slung across my shoulders.

"Jasmine be safe, Ima miss you" my sister sniffled as she just stared at me with sadness in her eyes. I didn't bother replying. I was too afraid my dad would hear all the commotion and wake up. If I was caught, I would certainly be going to school the next morning with a million bruises. I wasn't risking that happening. Minnie wanted to come with me but didn't wanna risk losing a good secretary job she had recently landed at a doctor's office. I jumped out of the second-floor window and crashed into the bushes. I laid sprawled across the grass trying desperately to move my body. I was certain I had bruised a few bones, but my adrenaline was too high to care about it. I managed to pull myself up and began sprinting down the block with my huge suitcase flopping behind me.

Once I got out of the window I ran, I ran like someone was chasing me. I ran until I couldn't anymore. I never knew why I was really running. Was I running away from myself or my dad? I ran until I could see the bus coming in the distance. I just knew I didn't want any of my past to be a part of my present.

I needed to get as far away as possible before someone saw a young teenage girl walking the streets at almost midnight. Dallas was not the place for me. Although I was seventeen and people probably wouldn't pay me any mind; I didn't want to take any chances. I was determined to get back to Chicago where I belonged, my home.

Over the past few months, I had gotten so depressed. I had completely changed as a person. I wasn't happy, and I damn sure felt like I didn't care about much anymore. I had endured my drunken father verbally, physically, and emotionally abusing me and my mother. I hated my sister for being older and being able to leave. See, when we moved to Dallas back in 2009 my sister was eighteen. At the first sign of trouble she ran.

I thought family was supposed to stick together but I guess not. Minnie was now twenty with no care in the world.

⸻

Four years ago, my mother came in and told us she was engaged to my dad, and we were moving to Dallas. Initially, I was excited. Who wouldn't want to move to Dallas? I loved the south. I had never been but the idea of leaving Chicago with its dirty streets and pissy hallways in the projects didn't sound like a bad idea. My dad had moved to Dallas a few years prior when I was nine to better his life.

I was attending Wilburg Preparatory. I was a freshman in high school. That year had been crazy for me. Coming into high school as a petite light skinned girl at only thirteen years old made me a target. I had skipped second grade about ten years ago, so I was usually always the youngest in my class. That was the year I lost my innocence and tried to keep it a secret. I had met a cute, tall, light skin freshman with short dreadlocks named Deon while walking to school. I had seen him a few times in school but was too shy to speak. I secretly had a crush on him. He was one of the popular kids from the neighborhood and I was the new kid on the block. We lived on the same block, so I saw him often, but we never spoke.

Humming music to myself, I tripped and fell on the sidewalk. A sea of papers were scattered across the grass as they had flown out of my bag when I fell. "Damn, you're clumsy" I heard a voice say as they were talking towards me, laughing. I looked up and my face turned bright red. It was my crush. He reached his hand out to help me and I was nervous to touch him. I grabbed his hand and my stomach fluttered. He was even cuter up close. He helped me stand up and scooped all my papers up from the ground. I just watched him, I felt stuck. I was mesmerized at his glowing skin. I looked him up and down and I felt different. He gave me a feeling that I had never had with anyone else. I wanted to hug him. I was young so I didn't really know what I was feeling. I stared at his juicy lips and imagined kissing him. We dated for a while until I left Chicago. I always remembered the sweet things he would say to me. One thing he always told me was "My love don't have an expiration date. No matter how long or how far, I'll always come back for you."

I rode the public city bus seated in the last row on the bus all the way to the Greyhound station. I tried to avoid windows and kept my head down just in case someone recognized me. Filled with paranoia, I looked over my shoulder constantly as I walked the few blocks to the station once I got off the bus. I kept feeling as if someone would recognize me and my entire plan would be ruined. Only once I got to the bus station, boarded the bus, and left Dallas that I began to relax a little. I traveled on the Greyhound for two days with only five dollars to my name, a bag of chips, two granola bars, and a small pack of crackers. I searched all around the house for days until it was time to leave and all I could come up with was five dollars. I had already pawned many of my electronics that mostly went unused to pay for my ticket. Anything else taken would make them suspicious.

I rode the same Greyhound bus for the most part until we got to Nebraska. I had to change buses once I got there and I began to have anxiety again. The bus officials in Nebraska were rude. The bus ride from Omaha, Nebraska to downtown Chicago was horrible. The bus was much more packed and scarier. Between crying babies and people that looked as if they were half-dead from a lifetime of smoking and drinking cursing at the bus driver for the lack of heat in the back of the bus, I just knew a fight would be breaking out soon. The bus driver ignored passengers request to turn up the heat and he even had the nerve to say he didn't care! I couldn't wait to get off the bus. I knew I would need at least a few dollars in my pocket once I got to Chicago, so I starved myself. Each day, I ate one thing once a day.

On the first day I ate a McDouble from McDonald's and a pop tart the next day. The first bus driver made a stop at McDonald's and I was given unopened food from passengers sitting around. It was easy, I kept staring with my sad face, and puppy dog eyes until people would feel bad enough and offer me some food. One lady was bold enough to ask me where my family was. I told her I was in Dallas visiting my dad and I was on my way back home to Chicago. She didn't question it.

One thing I knew how to do was survive due to the crazy streets of Chicago. At every stop, I was paranoid police officers were waiting to take me back to Dallas. I couldn't risk going back. If I went back, I knew I would be subject to constant beatings and 24/7 lockdown. The greyhound finally pulled into the bus station in downtown Chicago, I couldn't help but feel excited and ready to hit the streets. I was finally home, my real home, where my heart was at.

CHAPTER TWO

HOME

O nce I got off of the bus, I realized I didn't have anyone to pick me up from the bus station and I had no money to get back to my old neighborhood on the block. It was 7:45PM, I knew if I didn't call anyone soon no one would feel like coming out in the cold to pick me up. I found a sweet lady who worked at the Greyhound in Chicago who was nice enough to give me her bus pass because she didn't need it anymore. She told me she was hoping to get off early and make her way home on the bus, but she now had to work late. The bus card expired at 11:30PM; I had a few hours before it was useless. I made my way to the train station and hopped on the train and transferred to the 'Red Line.'

I knew I was close to home once I was greeted by the strong smell of urine, babies crying, and a hustler selling frooties, socks, and packs of face towels on the train. Frooties were small chewy candies often sold in the hood for pennies. They were commonly known as "penny candy."

I laughed to myself. Yeah, my city was crazy, there was a lot

of killing but no one could say that we lacked having true hustlers in

our city. People were getting money by any means necessary. I rode

the red line all the way to the last stop, 95th. I met a cute guy on the

train ride who flirted with me the entire time. He added me on

Facebook, and I told him I would hit him up once I got settled. When

I got off the train, the infamous windy city greeted me with an

intense slap of cold air. I began getting cold, I realized I only had on

two thin jackets.

I pulled my jackets tighter. I asked to use the boy's phone

who was flirting with me.

I called my old friend, Meka, and asked if her mom could

pick me up on 95th at the corner store. Meka's family used to be

close to my dad and we visited each other until my dad had a falling

out with them and they distanced themselves. I still liked them; I

chose not to let my dad's shenanigans fuck up the relationship I had

with Meka. She was like a cousin to me. "Hello!?" Meka answered

the phone sounding irritated. "Friend, what's good!?" I screamed into

the phone. "Bubbles? Is this my bitch Bubbles?" Bubbles was a

nickname only Meka called me. When I was younger, I was in love

with bubbles. She used to tease me about it by calling me bubbles

and the name stuck with me. "Yes, I'm home!" I hollered.

"OMG, girl I thought something happened I was expecting to

hear from you hours ago" she squealed. "No girl, my bus arrived late." I asked her if she could come pick me up and she agreed. I just had to wait thirty minutes for her to come. Meka was the only one I knew who had a license already at our age. She didn't have a car, but her mom let her drive it on occasions. Hanging up, I handed the cute guy back his phone and told him I was waiting for my ride. He offered to wait with me, but I told him I was a big girl and could handle it. "I'm going down the street to wait for them at the store because I'm hungry" I stated. "Alright, at least let me walk you down the street then I'll come back and get on my bus" he suggested.

I had been talking to him for the past forty-five minutes and never asked for his name nor did he ask for mine. Adding each other on Facebook didn't help because his name was 'El Chapo; BoutMyCash.' Niggas was always frontin' they move like they were big-time drug dealers or apart of the cartel. I couldn't say too much though because I used my middle name on social media, 'MarieLuvinMyself.' "Damn, you got a cute ass body" he smirked as he licked his lips. I was annoyed. Not only was this his fourth time giving me the same "compliment," I also hated when people told me that. It was degrading because often, niggas were only imagining fucking me. Being petite with a slight coke bottle shape and a big butt was a blessing and a curse. Sometimes I felt like I had no identity besides the pretty brown skin girl with the coke bottle shape. I wanted someone to like me for something else. I was no fool, I knew my body was what attracted people to me before anything else. "No, I can walk down the street by myself. I'll hit you up later. Make sure you don't miss your bus" I stated nonchalantly. He gave me a side hug and ran to catch his bus that was about to pull off.

I left the train station and walked down the street to the gas station. While I was at the gas station, I bought some *Hot Krunchy Kurls* and some *Now and Laters*, I hadn't had those in a long time. Dallas didn't have many corner stores or corner restaurants where you could walk in and order a 3-piece chicken wings, fries, and a pop with mild sauce on top for $2.99. I was in heaven as I scarfed down the snacks. I had been waiting for this moment.

My ears, hands and feet were freezing! I did not miss wintertime in Chicago. I knew I had to figure out a way to get a coat soon or I was going to end up with pneumonia. When Meka finally pulled up, I was almost sure my hands had frostbite. I hurried and got into the car so she could take me to my friend Amber's house.

I was so excited to be in Chicago I'd forgotten to call her. I also didn't remember her number. I didn't have access to any computer to get her number from Facebook. I gave them the address and prayed to God she was at the house because I hadn't talked to her in a few days, but she knew I was coming and assured her mom would allow me to stay with them.

We pulled up to the house, I told Meka I would link up with her later and made my way to the front door. I was nervous and scared to go in the house because I hadn't seen Amber in a long time. I didn't bother to ask to stay with Meka because her mom wouldn't allow me to stay with her knowing I was a runaway. She didn't like being involved in any drama. I also knew Amber's mom house was the meet up spot back in the day, so I knew I was bound to see people from our neighborhood in her house. I was excited to see my old home girls from the block but dreaded hearing about a blast from the past I was trying to forget about.

My old friends hadn't seen me in years. I was nervous because a few years back before I moved to Dallas, I started fucking with Amber's cousin Adonis, he stopped messing with me and I started flirting with his brother, Anthony, to piss him off. I caused them to fight and at the end of all that neither one of them were fucking with me and tried to get some girls to jump me.

Amber never stopped being friends with me over that, Amber always told me that wasn't any of her business and she wasn't gonna' end a six-year friendship over niggas. When I finally rang the doorbell, a random old man answered the door with an attitude, and I got scared. "Hi, is Amber here?" I asked.

"Who is you?" the old man questioned.

"I'm Jasmine, I was supposed to meet her here." I said.

"Aw I know who you are, Amber your friend at the door!" He hollered as he motioned for me to come in. I was still confused on who this man was.

As soon as Amber walked in the living room, she was talking shit. "Girl yo ass need some mo' meat on them bones, you need to eat!" she laughed.

"Bitch I do eat, and I don't wanna be fat, I just want more boobs then I would have everything niggas want" I spun around and flipped my hair full of micro braids, "yeah I'm that bitch!" I quickly pulled her to the side, "who is that old ass man? How he know me?" I asked. "Girl that's my uncle, he's staying with us for a while until he gets his own place." Amber laughed. "I told him I was expecting you to be coming soon." "I thought I was at the wrong house" I joked. Remember you sent me a message on Facebook a few days ago telling me when she you should be getting here?" she questioned. "Oh yeah, I remember" I stated.

We went upstairs to Amber's mom room to tell her I was there then I went and saw everybody there I hadn't seen in a while. The first night Amber's sister Angel, Nima and I stayed up talking and laughing. Nima's boyfriend, Jeremiah lived there with their two kids; two boys. Amber had one brother and two sisters but the house was always full with people from around the way.

Angel was cool to hang with, but she wasn't around a lot because she had responsibilities. Most nights she spent at her boyfriend's house. Angel was only eighteen years old with two kids already. I couldn't knock her though because I was out there getting it like she was, I was just lucky enough to not get pregnant. God knew I didn't need a child right now.

Around 1 AM, we were turnt' smoking and laughing when a familiar face from my old neighborhood, Marcus, had walked in. I had known Marcus since he was in 3rd grade when he was a scrawny kid who no one messed with. As soon as he walked in, I couldn't keep my eyes off him. Marcus had on some all-black True Religion jeans, an all-black V-neck t-shirt, wheat Tims, and a black Oakland Raiders fitted cap. I also noticed he had a full sleeve of tattoos on his left arm. He looked good. His smooth chocolate skin looked so good. He came in, gave me a hug, and nodded what's up to everyone.

When he left the room, I blurted out "Damn, he done glowed up! Marcus is cute now and he look like he got a lil' swag now."

"Girl yes, he ain't no lil' boy no more, he in the field now" Nima stated. I knew what that meant, Marcus was in the streets and he was more than likely drillin' niggas.

Amber laughed, "girl I know you better not think he cute, he too crazy and young for you." Marcus was only two years younger than me but that wasn't bad. I laughed to myself. I had already made up my mind that I was gonna take my chance.

"What's he doing here so late anyway?" I asked. "His moms back in prison for stealing a car; you know she back on drugs now. He been staying with us for about three months now since they were evicted" she replied. "Damn, that's sad" I replied. We laughed and joked 'til our eyes were crossing from sleepiness and we dozed off to sleep.

I woke up feeling good about myself. There were a lot of voices outside of Amber's room. I walked out to use the bathroom to see Adonis. Adonis was from my old neighborhood and he didn't like me. A few years back he dedicated himself to making sure everyone in the hood knew I was a bitch that I wasn't shit, a hoe, and I couldn't be trusted.

Adonis was the best friend of Tevin. Tevin was a guy I used to mess with from my old middle school. I used to have a big crush on Tevin a few years back, we started flirting and messing around with each other. We did innocent things like kissing and him slapping my ass. Josh was two years older than me and wanted to do more than that. Moral of the story is that I didn't want to do more than that and he made it a point to lie and let everyone know I gave him an STD. In return, I had my big cousins catch him leaving school one day and had them beat him so bad he landed in the hospital for a few days. I had to leave our old hood for a while after that.

Adonis tried to run my name through the mud every chance he got. To my surprise, Adonis got up, hugged me and said, "Damn girl, you done grew up, you look good as fuck." I blushed.

Now suddenly, this nigga fuck with me because he sees my ass done glowed up. Niggas; I sighed.

I made my way back to Amber's room after I used the bathroom. I couldn't get back to sleep so I decided to wait until she got up. While I waited, I decided to use her laptop to hop on Facebook and see what was going down on the book. Back in Dallas, my dad took my phone every other month and this was one of those times I didn't have my phone.

As soon as I logged on, I kept receiving notifications. I had thirteen messages in my inbox, and they were all from my family. I opened a message from my mom that said she knew I was in Chicago, she wanted me to call her, so she knew I was alright and to go meet my grandmother.

I wanted to see my grandmother, but I didn't want to be forced to stay over there and I wasn't about to let anyone control me and make me stay in the house. I had called my other family members to stay with them, but no one wanted to help me when I needed the help. People only talked like they wanted to help you. I couldn't bear to stay with my grandma. I had stayed with my grandmother before I left Chicago and was almost stuck with a dirty needle left behind by one of my drugged-out older cousins. I had dug into my bag of clothes looking for a school uniform and had found an old used rusty needle.

I made a quick little status *I'm Home! Where y'all at? Who wanna' come see me? Y'all know I couldn't stay away for long!*

When Amber finally woke up, I told her I was about to go see some of my family and try to get some money to buy me a coat. I wasn't worried about hiding once I got to Chicago because it's a big city and it would be difficult for my family to get to me out here.

I called my grandmother before I left Amber's house and told her I was on my way to see her. She told me to meet her at church and that she was happy to hear from me and was worried about me. She asked where I was staying at, but I just stated a friend's house. I knew that was a setup, she only wanted to know so she could pick me up and try to keep me at her house.

I had made up my mind and knew I wasn't going to be staying at her house. I wanted to live somewhere I could get up and go whenever I wanted and where people wouldn't constantly tell me what to do. Amber's mom didn't bother you as long as you didn't bother her, steal from her, and cleaned up after yourself. That was perfect for me.

It felt good walking to the bus stop and knowing another bus was coming within the next five to ten minutes. I hated waiting for a bus in Dallas because the buses ran every twenty to thirty minutes. I took in all the action around me.

Niggas posted in front of the candy store, they were either selling drugs, waiting to catch somebody slipping, or on the lookout for somebody. Niggas was tryna to holla' at me as I walked down the street but none of them were cute enough for me to stop and entertain. That's one of the things I missed about Chicago. Niggas was bold, they would try to holla' at you no matter who was around.

They had this *IDGAF, I'm that nigga* type of attitude, and I loved it.

The 55th street bus pulled up three minutes after I arrived at the bus stop. I rode the bus all the way to Halsted from there I took the #8 Halsted bus all the way up to 63rd. Once I got off the bus, I ran into my old friend, Bre, who lived nearby.

Bre was my old friend from Wilburg Preparatory back in the day. We used to have lunch lit' every day when we were together. I took her number and told her we would link up a little later. As I walked the three blocks to my grandma's church, I was a bit nervous. I hadn't seen my pastor in years and ever since I moved to Dallas I hadn't really been into church or God.

I felt like God didn't like or care about me since he didn't take me and my mom from that situation. He just left us, but I couldn't judge because I had left my mom too. When I got to the church, I mingled with everybody, but my mind wasn't there. I felt uncomfortable because I wasn't properly dressed and didn't belong, I felt like the devil sitting inside God's house.

I had done so much wrong shit and I hadn't been to church in over two years. I wanted to stop by Zavion's house later, a nigga I went to school and kept in contact with who said I could stay with him. I was trying to make him mine. I needed a nigga with money who could take care of me. He was perfect since he had money and his own apartment. Zavion was a few years older than me. During school, I always hung around the older kids. I didn't plan on staying with Amber's family forever. I was ready to make moves and get to the money. I said I wanted to take my chance with Marcus but that was only temporary. Marcus was a little boy. I just wanted to flirt and chill with him; nothing more. I had my eye on a few niggas, but I had to keep my options open. Zavion was a grown man and about his money.

May the best man win, I thought.

Angel was throwing a kickback later today at the house, so I wasn't trying to be out late so I wouldn't miss it. I still needed time to change clothes and freshen up again. I didn't know who would be at the kickback, so I had to be prepared. I finally told my grandma I was leaving around five pm, just as I expected, she wouldn't let me leave. I shook my head; I knew she would have some trick up her sleeve to make sure I stayed with her. She said she didn't want me taking the bus in the cold and at night.

The church gathering was over, but everyone was preparing to eat dinner there in the basement, a tradition done almost every week. My grandmother's church was like a close-knit family. They did almost everything together. My grandma kept trying to get me to stay for dinner, so I did. We walked to the store while dinner was being prepped. "You shole' is sneaky to run away to a whole other state all the way across the country girl" my grandma stated.

I laughed, "Well I'm living up to my name since y'all always call me sneaky."

"How you gone enroll in school?" she asked.

"I was hoping mommy would give you guardianship, so you can enroll me." I quipped.

"Girl I ain't in no shape or condition to take guardianship of no child." She said shaking her head.

"You don't have to take care of me, I will get a job and pay for everything myself, I just need you to get me in school." I pleaded. Even though my life was fucked up and I had fucked up ways, my mom made sure I knew education was important.

"Hmmm, well I ain't got no problem with it but we'll see what your mom says." I loved my grandma because she was the only one that understood me. I was finally dropped off back at Amber's after I convinced my grandma I was in good hands. Before I got out the car my grandma gave me her 'government phone' so she would be able to reach me, or I could reach her if anything happened. I was happy because I needed to hit my home girls to see what was poppin' later that week.

Walking into the house NuNu was all over me before I could blink twice. "Jas! OMG, girl you were the last person I expected to see. Girl you so damn pretty! I missed you!" NuNu, whose real name was Unique, was a real thick and funny girl. I didn't like her when I first met her but over time, I got to know her and grew to love her.

The rest of the night I chilled at the kickback and mingled with everyone. It was nothing but shit talking, games of Spades, laughs, and good vibes. After I grew a bit tired, I went to Amber's room to get away from the crowd. Marcus walked in looking good in some roc jeans and a fresh wife beater. He sat down next to me, watching my phone while I was texting. "Damn, can I get some privacy with your nosey ass?" I asked sarcastically. I was smiling so he knew I wasn't serious.

"Shut up lil' girl, what you in here doing?" he asked.

I smirked, "Lil girl? Lil boy stay in your place, ain't nothing about me a lil' girl." Marcus and I stayed in the room the rest of the night flirting with each other, we even fell asleep in Amber's bed together.

I can't lie and say I didn't want that to happen. When I woke up in the middle of the night and realized I was in the bed with him, I scooted my ass back up against him so I could feel him. I didn't too much care for him, but I did enjoy his company. I was lonely.

Damn, did Amber see this? I thought.

I woke up in Amber's bed and Marcus was cuddled up behind me around 7AM. Earlier, I didn't even care if Amber or anyone else had walked in and seen us. He must be feeling me like I'm feeling him. I hurried and got out of the bed, so I could get ready for my day. I wondered where Amber had slept since we were in her bed.

That was just us falling asleep talking. It wasn't nothing more than that. I thought.

I walked out of the room in search of where Amber had slept last night. I found her in the living room sprawled across the couch.

Everyone else was still asleep which gave me time to get in the shower and get dressed. After putting on some dark blue jeans that looked as if they were painted on, a cute tan fitted V-neck, and some all-white force ones, I threw my hair up in a bun and glossed my lips up. I put on a coating of Carmex and 2 coatings of Smackers lip gloss that smelled like strawberries as I was leaving out, Amber woke up and I told her I was going to one of my old home girl's house.

"It's too cold, I'm not going anywhere so I'll see you later" she stated sleepily.

I chucked up the deuces sign, smiled and was out the door. Once I got to the bus stop, I called Meka and told her I was on my way. I walked to Cottage Grove and rode two buses and a train for almost two hours to the west side. Chicago was a big city and sometimes it took a while to get to the other side of town. Once I got off the bus, I spotted a Citi Trends just down the street. I walked down the block to Citi Trends to see how much money I needed for a coat. I knew I was bound to get sick since I only had a thick bomber jacket to keep me warm.

I found a stylish all-black pea coat at the back of the store that resembled the ones celebrity women wore often. I knew it wasn't an expensive one like the celebrities, but you didn't have to spend money to look like you had money. It was only twenty dollars, but I didn't even have that. I was broke. I looked around and notice only two workers. One was working the cash register and the other was hanging clothes on the rack. I found my size, slipped the coat on, and walked out of the door. I was in survival mode and had to do whatever to take care of myself. I'd done worse before. I looked back a few times to ensure no one was following me as I walked the few blocks over to Meka's neighborhood.

I walked through the buildings to get to Meka's side of the building. It was quiet outside; I knew that was only because it was cold. It was two degrees outside today. I playfully made a beat on Meka's door until it swung open. "Hey Bubbles" Meka happily greeted as she opened the door.
It was turnt as soon as I walked in Meka's house. Rakia and Ziana ran up to me as soon as I stepped through the door. They were blasting Chicago juke music like they were having a full-blown house party. Rakia got in my face, "Bitch where you been at? You been missing in action since you touched down in the Chi!"

"Girl I been around, I'm tryna' see everybody before I

disappear on all y'all ass. I'm tryna get this money!" "Gee, let me use your phone to call my uncle because my minutes are almost gone." I dialed my uncle Greg. "Hey Uncle Greg!"

"Who is this?" he asked

"This is Jasmine, Nicole's daughter."

"Oh, girl I didn't know that was you. Wassup? How you been?"

"I'm fine Uncle Greg, I was calling to let you I was in Chicago, I wanted to stop by and see you."

"What you doing in Chicago? Is your mom here too?"

"No, it's just me Uncle Greg, I'm supposed to be finishing school up here." He agreed to give me some money after talking with him a few minutes and explaining what was going on.

"Ok, well come visit me tomorrow at my job. I got a lot of things to do today and I don't have time" he stated.

"Okay, I'll do that, TTYL" I remarked.

The rest of the day I chilled with Meka, and Rakia. Rakia was Meka's younger sister. Rakia was wild and always wanted to roll with us. Rakia was only fourteen, but she always tried to sneak into parties with us. Meka's mom finally came home from work and brought us some chicken wings and fries from the corner restaurant. I was happy; the fries and the chicken wings were drenched in mild sauce. "Bitch, this food bomb! Dallas don't know nothing about this shit!" I exclaimed.

"I heard them bitches were some birds, they all conceited like Jas" Meka's sister, Ziana stated. Everyone burst out laughing.

I spun around, "Y'all bitches mad because I'm cute and thick" I stated jokingly.

"Girl I'm thicker than you, sit down." Meka laughed.

"Y'all bitches always hating!" I stuck out my middle finger.

It was about nine o' clock PM and I was ready to leave. I waited until Meka was ready to take me home. Meka borrowed her mom's car and drove me back to Amber's house. "Gee hit me up tomorrow so we can figure out what we gonna' do later this week." Meka said hugging me.

"Alright." Meka wanted to go out sometime that week and I was down with it. I needed to find me some niggas.

CHAPTER THREE

Games People Play

When I walked into Amber's house, I saw a familiar face. Brian Jr from my old neighborhood, the Heights, along with another boy I didn't recognize but he was fine. I tried not to stare, I knew someone in the house would catch on and be messy. Brian Jr, who's better known as BJ, started smiling and gave me a hug. "Wassup shorty?"

"Damn, you remember me? I ain't think you would even remember" I replied. BJ was a short and stocky caramel skinned funny guy. He resembled Romeo without the braids; he was a cutie.

"Jas, yeah I remember yo lil' ass." His friend started laughing. I did an awkward ass wave and said hey. BJ noticed,

"Aw my fault, sis this my nigga Tyrek, Tyrek this Jas. She lived in the Heights with us back in the day."

"Wassup?" I replied. In my head I was thinking, *'Fuck your*

35

name, when you gone be mine?' I had to get away from him fast because daddy had me ready to risk it all for him. Tyrek had skin the color of cocoa, a slight beard growing in, and he was muscular. He was the whole package besides being a bit short. You could tell he spent a lot of time in the gym. I zeroed in on his manhood, it was bulging, and I was curious. His hair was the true definition of being seasick with his waves. He even smelled good! "What's good shorty?" he replied with a slight smile. I blushed; his perfect white teeth made him even finer.

"Jas your ass finally back! Come in the room with us." Amber said looking from the doorway. I excused myself and walked in Amber's room. Angel, Nima, and a new caramel skinned girl with long curly hair was in the room. Amber introduced me to the caramel-skinned girl. "Jas this my friend Keisha, Keisha this Jas." Keisha looked as if she could be mixed with Hispanic.

By midnight, it was nothing but good vibes between all of us. We cracked jokes, talked about old times living on J block, and played spades. A little after midnight, BJ, Tyrek, and Jeremiah came in the room and we were turnt the rest of the night. BJ cracked jokes the entire night, he was funny, but my attention was still on Tyrek's fine ass.

At 2 AM, BJ and Tyrek finally went home and Jeremiah and Nima went to bed. Angel had gone to bed shortly after midnight Keisha was leaving out the door. As soon as everyone left, Amber began bragging about Tyrek. "Girl you seen my baby? He's so fine, everything he does, he makes it look good."

I was a bit quiet because I was jealous she was talking about him like that. I really wanted to know if she was fucking with him or just had a harmless crush. "Y'all talk?" "Yeah, we talk off and on. He plays too many games though."

"What you mean by that? Shit, you let him smash?" I tried to say it in a playful way, so they wouldn't think I was just being nosy.

I didn't want her to know I liked him so I played it cool.

"Girl no, I ain't let him smash, he gotta do more than just kiss me to get the goodies."

"True", I agreed with Amber.

I rolled my eyes and started laughing. Jackpot, that's all I needed to know. If they weren't official then he was for anybody, including me. I smirked then we ended up talking and reminiscing about the old days. We ended up going to sleep around 4 AM.

I woke up to Marcus touching me. "Aye Jas?" he called as he nudged me.

I could barely open my eyes. I felt around the room looking for my phone. "What?"

"Let me get one of these blankets you're sleeping with."

"Boy you're waking me up at 5 AM about a blanket?" I asked irritated. He started laughing. "It's cold out here on the couch" he stressed. I got up and gave him one of the blankets I was sleeping on and walked to the bathroom.

On my way back to the room, I peeped in the living room and saw Marcus watching TV, laid up on the couch. I smirked and made a devilish grin. I walked in the living room and told Marcus to move over. I wanted to show him I was feeling him. He looked at me, smirked, and scooted over for me. I sat down close to him. I began rubbing my body faking like I was cold.

"You cold?" he asked. I smirked, either this nigga just dumb and falling for all the traps or he was feeling me like I was feeling him. I looked at him with puppy dog eyes and replied "yes."

He opened his cover and let me get under with him. I leaned back on him and pretended to watch TV.

I tried to sneak and look at him, as soon as I looked up, he was looking at me, smirking. We stared at each other for about thirty seconds then our lips greeted each other, and our tongues intertwined.

I caressed his chest while he slowly laid me on my back on the couch as we kissed. He tugged at my pajama shorts and attempted to untie them, but I stopped him. I wasn't feeling him like that yet.

"We gotta do this somewhere else, anybody can walk in here and its 6 AM." He stated breathing into my ear.

"I'm sleepy anyway, let's see where this goes another time" I suggested.

"Please" Marcus begged.

"Look, I'm going to bed. We'll try this again another night." I concluded.

"You sure? I can find a place, just give me a few minutes." He pleaded.

"No, I'm going to bed." I retorted. The more and more he was talking, the more he was looking like a lame ass nigga in my eyes.

That's what I get for tryna mess with a lil' ass boy, he doesn't even know how to play the game and be cool. Ugh. I went back in Amber's room and went to sleep.

The sound of the phone vibrating on the nightstand woke me. "Hello?" I said sleepily rubbing the grit from my eyes

"Hello! What are you doing still sleep at 10:30 AM?"

"Grandma, it's not even late in the day. You're calling super early."

"It is late. You need to be up and be doing something productive with yourself anyway."

"Grandma, I would be able to if you let me get enough rest."

"Don't get sarcastic with me, write this number down and call your cousin. Ashley wants to see you"

I sat up, "She does? Where does she stay at?"

"She's at Mary's house." Mary was a friend of my grandmothers from my childhood church.

"Okay, I'll call her grandma."

"Alright now,' make sure you call her so y'all can see each other."

"Alright, I'll call you back later grandma."

"Alright, talk to you later'."

I went back to sleep; I could barely keep my eyes open. Amber was still sleep anyway. When I woke again it was 1:45 in the afternoon, I needed to get up and get dressed. I woke up feeling little embarrassed about what happened between me and Marcus a few hours ago.

I walked out of Amber's room and instantly caught eyes with Marcus on the computer. He still looked good, even though he had annoyed this morning. I made my way to the bathroom, did my business then walked in the kitchen. "Good Morning, what you cooking?" Amber was in the kitchen cooking breakfast or I should say lunch.

"Hey, eggs, bacon and waffles."

"Can I have some?"

"Yea, if it's enough."

"Alright, what you got planned for today?"

Amber shrugged her shoulders, "Shit, I might go to my friend house."

I playfully hit her on the thigh, "Friend?" What friend, it's a boy?"

She started laughing, "Girl it ain't even like that."

"Mhm" I gave her a look like I knew she was lying. Marcus walked in, stole a piece of bacon, and tried to run. Whack! Amber slapped Marcus dead across the back of his neck.

Marcus turned around angry, "What the fuck you do that for?"

Amber smirked, "Stop stealing my food. Make your own shit!" I smirked, I low-key felt like he deserved the shit but mostly because he was acting strange earlier.

After eating, I took a shower and got dressed. I was leaving when I heard BJ's loudmouth ass talking shit. I heard him in Jeremiah and Nima's room. I walked back to the room, I wanted to see if he brought Tyrek with him because I was looking good.

I knocked on the door and Nima let me in. "What's up light bright?" BJ said.

"Wassup?" I got happy when I saw Tyrek, he nodded his head at me, I smiled and waved. I was happy I was looking good, good thing he didn't see me when I first woke up. I sat down for a lil' bit right across from Tyrek. I needed to be on my way to see my cousin, Ashley, but I couldn't pass up any opportunities with Tyrek. I acted like I was all in the conversation, BJ and Jeremiah were roasting each other and talking about where they were from.

Truth be told, I didn't see either one of them as a gangsta' but that was my opinion. I purposely kept looking at Tyrek, I knew I would catch his eye eventually. He finally looked at me. *"Got him!"* I thought. After that, he kept looking at me. When I caught him looking at me, I would smile and look away but not before I made it known I was checking for him. We played this game for about ten minutes and he kept smiling at me.

"Man, I gotta piss," Tyrek stated. Tyrek got up and went to the bathroom, I waited about three minutes and got up too. "I'm about to leave y'all, I'll be back later."

"Where you going?" Nima asked.

"I'm going to go see my cousin then I'm going downtown to get some money from my uncle."

"Oh, alright." Nima stated.

I walked out and ran dead into Tyrek in the living room. I brushed up on him on purpose, we were the only ones in the room and Amber's room door was closed. I smiled, "You're 'bout to go say hi to your girl?"

"Man, what? That ain't my girl." he countered.

His attitude changed quick.

I threw my hands up; surrendering, "My bad, I only assumed that because that's how she's making it seem. Maybe you should let that be known." I smirked, I was being disloyal, but I didn't care. I figured she didn't need to know. He was up for grabs.

He looked at me and smirked, "You good shorty, shit I might be tryna put you on my team." He yapped.

I laughed, "Yo' team? Nigga, you fuck with me and I'll be the only one you would want on your team."

"Alright, well show me then. Put your number in my phone." I took his phone and put the number to my grandmother's government phone in there. As soon as I was giving him his phone back, Amber's door opened. I ran and sat down at the computer like I was occupied.

Amber walked out smiling, "Hey Tyrek. Jas, I thought you was gone."

I turned around, "Aw yeah, I'm about to leave. I needed to send my cousin a message on Facebook, so I don't use up the minutes on my phone."

"Alright, be safe."

Be safe was something everyone told each other in Chicago. The streets were vicious, and you never knew if you would be seeing one of your homies or family members on the nine o' clock news.

I logged into Facebook, sent my cousin a quick message letting her know I was on my way and put on my jackets to leave. "Alright y'all, I'm gone. See y'all later."

BJ walked in the room, "Where you going big head? What way?"

"I'm 'bout to go see my cousin then go get some money from

my uncle so downtown then up North."

"Shit, I'm 'bout to get up outta' here too. Where she stay at?"

"She stay up North, you don't need the exact address stalker" I teased.

"Alright hold up, we're headed that way too, so we'll go with you."

"Alright, hurry up, I was supposed to leave over an hour ago." Inside, I was rejoicing. This was my time to get Tyrek to myself. BJ told Tyrek they were leaving, and we all left out. We got to the bus stop in about two minutes. BJ cracked jokes the entire time we were waiting for the bus.

"Aye, how your cousin look? Is she cute? And, don't lie just because she's your cousin." BJ said.

"Boy, you got my cousin fucked up! She is bad!"

"Alright, we 'bout to go with you." BJ advised.

We rode the 55th bus to Jefferson to the 'Red Line' then hopped on the train headed up North. Once we got off the train and our last bus, I realized it was getting late, it was five o' clock in the afternoon. I hoped Mary would still let Ashley come out. We were three houses down, but I didn't want Mary to assume we were just trying to get out to be with some niggas. She could be overbearing sometimes. "Y'all wait right here while I go get her. I don't want them getting concerned when they see y'all."

"Why we can't go? They don't wanna' meet some real

niggas?" BJ joked.

Me and Tyrek looked at each other and laughed.

"You doing too much. Just stay here while I go get her" I groaned.

I rang the doorbell and waited for someone to answer. The door opened and Mary appeared in the doorway. I hadn't seen her in years, she now looked like she should be called *Big Mama*. "Hi Miss Mary, is Ashley here?" She was sweet but wasn't about any bullshit. "And, who are you?"

"Oh, I'm her cousin, Jasmine. I think you attended my grandmother's church sometimes." I was caught off guard by her smart-ass question. She attended my grandmother's church occasionally; she had seen me there with my grandmother.

"Bitch you know who I am" I mumbled to myself.

Ashley and I shared a grandmother. She had to know who I was.

"Oh yeah, I'm Mary. I remember you; I'm sorry chile'. As you get older, you start to forget things and ya' vision gets bad" she rattled.

"Oh, I understand" I responded.

"Oh, okay let me get Ashley for you." I rolled my eyes as soon as she turned around, I did not like her vibe. Ashley came to the door. I smiled; my attitude changed.

"Hey Ashley! We got so much to talk about!" I exclaimed.

"I know, I missed you" she remarked.

"I missed you too. How long you gone----"

"How long will you be having her out? When will she be back here?" Mary interrupted asking.

Miss Mary had come back to the door and cut me off. I was seriously getting annoyed by her. She had this look on her face like I was scum or beneath her. I felt like I could've been the gum on the bottom of her shoe. I stared at her, mean mugging but didn't say anything. "Well?" She crossed her arms over her chest her patience wearing thin.

"Um, I guess I'll have her back by eleven o' clock."

"No, how about ten?" I knew she meant that as an order, rather than a question by the way she said it.

"Okay, I'll have her here by ten."

"Alright, you ladies be safe. Ashley call me if you need anything." I didn't like how she was treating me. Maybe I was some reckless teenage runaway that was always getting into some trouble, but she still didn't have a right to judge me.

After making sure Mary went back into the house, Ashley and I walked down a few houses to meet up with BJ and Tyrek.

"Damn, it took y'all long enough" BJ said.

"Shit, that was the lady. She was doing the most. I low-key wanted to curse her ass out. She was tryna talk to me like I was some random bitch off the street" I explained.

"I know right, I don't why she was acting like that. I mean ain't nothing gone happen to me. You're my cousin." Ashley agreed.

"Right but fuck her. Let's get downtown so I can get this money from Uncle Greg" I stated.

"Alright, let's go" BJ said.

We piled on the bus and headed downtown. Ashley and I sat in seats next to each other and BJ and Tyrek sat right behind us. BJ popped my bun, "Damn girl, this all your hair?"

"Hell yea, it's all my hair. Why wouldn't it be?" I asked.

"Shit, bitches be lying. They be putting a whole bundle of weave in a bun to make it seem like it's they shit" he stated laughing.

I laughed, "Well shit, I ain't one of them. My shit is real, it's all mine" I retorted.

"Aye, let's switch seats. Let your cousin come back here and Tyrek sit up there with you." BJ suggested.

I rolled my eyes, "Mhm, you think you slick. You feelin' my cousin ain't you?" I asked snickering.

"Hell yea" he stated smiling. I turned around like I had an attitude, but I really didn't. I only hoped that Ashley was feelin' BJ at least a little bit so I could get some time with Tyrek.

"Ashley, you wanna switch seats and sit back there with BJ?"

"Yea baby, come back here. I ain't gone hurt you or nothing" BJ proclaimed. I rolled my eyes,

"Ashley don't listen to him, It's your choice." She laughed,

"Jas it's cool, I'll sit back there with him" she replied.

"Alright" I cheered. Once we switched seats, I went back to seeming unbothered. I looked out the window, hoping that Tyrek would make the first move. I was looking out the window for about five minutes getting agitated. Tyrek finally nudged me, "move over."

"Move over? Who you talking to like that?" I retaliated. I looked over at him and noticed he was smiling so I knew he was playing. I'm glad he wasn't serious because I was about to trip with him. This was the start of a new friendship, or at least I thought. The rest of the ride Tyrek and I rambled on about ourselves to get to know each other.

Our stop was coming up. I turned around to tell BJ and Ashley to get ready to get off and I was greeted with them lip locking like they were ready to pounce on each other right on the bus. I was shocked. "Damn, y'all ain't waste no time, I said.

I turned to Tyrek and we both burst into laughter. Ashley looked embarrassed. "Don't trip I told her. I'm not gone tell nobody, you good" I reassured her. The rest of the night Ashley and BJ were boo'd up. We got off the bus and walked to the Ritz-Carlton hotel, where Uncle Greg worked. I stopped before we all walked in. "Now before we go in here don't embarrass me and try to tone down ya' hood mentalities. Leave that shit outside, my uncle ain't like that" I declared.

"What? He some typa' butterball bean pie type of nigga?" BJ asked. Everyone burst out laughing.

"Nigga fuck you, just be cool alright" I retorted.

"Alright man, it's whatever he said holding his hands up" surrendering.

"Yeah, alright" I said.

CHAPTER FOUR

Troubled Waters

H i, I'm here to see Greg Williams, from Security." I asked the tall Caucasian lady at the hotel's front desk.

"And, may I ask who you are, so I can let him know?" she asked.

"Oh, I'm his niece, Jasmine."

"Okay, go ahead and have a seat, he'll be right down" she assured.

"Okay, thank you" I said. We sat down and listened to BJ talk shit about everyone that was unfortunate enough to have to walk past us.

"Now look at this bow tie and a bean pie ass nigga. He looking like *'Topflight'* around this motherfucker."

I started laughing. I looked up, and noticed it was my uncle walking towards us.

"Boy you got my uncle fucked up," I said. "That's yo' uncle?

He outta' line for that" he said. Everybody started laughing.

"It's his uniform, don't come for him" I defended.

"Shit, that don't matter. He still can have on a uniform and put his own swag to it" BJ said.

"Hey Uncle Greg!" I chirped as I gave him a hug.

"How you been sweetheart?" he asked.

"I been good, just need some winter clothes before I get sick" I stated.

"Yeah, I see that. We don't want you to get pneumonia out here." Uncle Greg turned around and shook hands with BJ, Ashley, and Tyrek. My uncle Greg wasn't familiar with Ashley because he was never around while we were growing up. He was the uncle who only came around during major holidays and even that had only recently started. I was embarrassed because BJ was making fun of my uncle when he turned his back, and I had suspicions Uncle Greg had saw him. I didn't want my uncle thinking I hung with these types of niggas even though they were the type of niggas I liked. It wasn't like I had much of a choice, those were the only type of niggas I seemed to attract anyway.

"Alright baby girl, be safe. Here's the money, I'll talk to you later. I gotta get back to work." He handed me a sealed envelope.

This man too official. He even sealed the envelope, I thought.

"Alright, thank you Uncle Greg. I love you and I'll call you tomorrow" I said. I didn't wanna be rude so I waited until I walked away to see how much money he gave me.

A hundred dollars!? He only gave me a hundred dollars. Damn, I have to find a cheap outfit for New Years, I thought.

He gave me a mixture of tens, fives, and ones, which made it seem like a lot of money, but it wasn't. *I'll make the best of it,* I figured. I folded all the money and tucked it into my bra.

"Alright Jas, where we going now?" BJ asked. "Ashley, you ready to go home?" I asked.

"No, I'll stay with y'all. Ain't nun' to do at her house. I've been bored in the house everyday" she admitted.

"She told me to have you home by ten. It's already 9 something. You sure?" I questioned.

"Yeah, I'm sure." Alright Ashley don't get me in trouble or have her trippin' with me over you" I warned.

"I got you, I'll tell her we got stuck downtown" she reassured.

"No, I really think you should go back" I objected.

"No, I wanna stay with y'all" she countered.

"Jas, stop being a hater. You heard her, she wanna stay with us. Plus let me get acquainted with my new boo. BJ chimed in. Ashley blushed.

"Alright, I ain't trippin,' I just don't want her to get in trouble"
I explained.

Ashley smiled at me, "Don't worry I'm good and they know you
gone look out for me anyway" she spluttered.

"Alright, fuck it. Let's go to my house" Tyrek said.

"Where you live at?" I asked.

"Over on 35th and Prairie" he replied.

"The low end!? That's my old hood."

"Aw yeah? I just moved down there, not too long ago."

"Yeah, I used to live on Michigan. Alright, we're going to
your house. Let's hurry up and go, it's cold!" I exclaimed.

We walked back to the bus stop and climbed on the bus. The
entire ride to the low-end, we were all boo'd up. Tyrek had his
tongue down my throat damn near the entire ride. He even sucked on
my neck and had me ready to drop my pants for him right there on
the bus.

I sat turned in my seat towards Tyrek with my legs on him. I
unbuckled my pants and let him find my warmth and explore it with
his hands. I tried to cover up what we were doing by putting a
shopping bag in front of us that Ashley had given me when we left
Miss Mary's house. It was full of snacks and I was the last one
eating out of the bag, so I was stuck with it.

I didn't put too much effort in trying to cover up because I didn't care if people knew. Older people were looking at us with disgust, but I didn't care. I was doing me, and nobody could do anything about it. I looked at him and smiled. He slipped one finger in and was greeted with my warm, wet stickiness on his fingers. He slowly pumped in and out then entered two fingers. He began pumping inside of me quicker and harder, I let out a slight moan. "Don't start something you can't finish" I teased.

He smirked, "I can finish it, you probably can't handle it" he countered.

"Is that a threat? Nigga you ain't ready for this pussy!" I exclaimed.

He laughed, "Alright, we'll see."

He slowly slid his hands out of me and wiped them off on the seat. I slid my leg down, turned around and seen Ashley and BJ tonguing each other down. I smirked. "Looks like they're having as much fun as we are" I smirked.

We got off the bus on 35thand King Dr and walked down to 35th and Prairie. As we walked to Tyrek house, I felt a twinge of sadness and excitement because this neighborhood was my old stomping grounds. I smiled to myself. *Memories.* I reminisced the rest of the way of the old crazy times I had. This was the same hood I met Deon in. The same block where I ran into him and was full of embarrassment from dropping my school papers.

Once we walked in Tyrek's house I was in complete awe. The house was surprisingly very clean and decorated so nicely in coral and grey. The living room was decorated with orangish-pinkish and grey drapes. There was a grey sectional couch that wrapped around the room topped off with coral plush pillows. I immediately tried to put my plan in action. Everyone went into Tyrek 's room while I started wandering around his house acting like I was looking for stuff, but it was only a set up. I figured Tyrek would eventually come looking for me which would get me alone with him while Ashley and BJ did their thang. We had plenty of time to ourselves since Tyrek's father wasn't around and his mom worked overnight shifts as security at the Sears tower downtown.

I stopped when I got back to the living room. I plopped down on the couch and pretended I was doing something important in my phone. Like clockwork, Tyrek came strolling down the hallway with his size twelve Tims smacking against the hardwood floor, he stopped at the entrance and leaned against the wall. "What you doing in here?" he asked.

"Nothing, I'm bored" I said. He walked over and sat so close to me that I could smell his minty gum he was chewing.

"You bored? Shit, I got something for us to do" he smirked.

"Oh yea? What's that?" I asked.

He laughed, "You're about to see." He got on top of me while I laid back on the couch. He kissed me then slid his hand up my shirt and caressed my breasts. I groped his penis through his pants until I got excited, I couldn't take it anymore. Tyrek lifted my bra up, sucked on my breast and twirled his tongue around my nipples until they were rock hard. I felt like being a lil' nasty. I sat up a little bit, "I want some gum." He looked at me confused.

"This the only piece I got" he explained.

"Okay, give me that piece in yo' mouth then" I dared. He smiled, leaned down and proceeded to push the gum in my mouth with his tongue. Once I had the gum, I held his tongue in my mouth and sucked on it. The kissing and sucking was so passionate that we were damn near trying to rip each other clothes off after that.

I unbuckled his pants and let his penis free. He slowly slid his tongue in my mouth and met my tongue. I let his fingers run down my torso until he met my belt buckle. We paused shortly while he unbuckled my pants and inserted one finger in pussy. I let his finger explore my pussy while he sucked on my neck. He inserted two fingers while I massaged his penis. I abruptly stopped. As bad as I wanted to fuck him, I didn't want to do it on the couch and with him only whipping his penis out and not taking off his clothes. It just made me feel like a hoe. Yes, I know it's ironic for me to say that, considering prior events.

"What's wrong?" he asked.

"I just don't wanna' have sex in here, like this" I explained. He smacked his lips,

"Jas, you trippin.' What's wrong with right here?" I frowned; he was starting to piss me off. It was too early for him to show his fuck boy tendencies.

You just might not get the pleasure of getting some of my

goodies. I said to myself.

"What you mean?" I stated smacking my lips like a typical ghetto girl from the Southside of Chicago. "We're in the living room in the open where my cousin or BJ can walk in anytime. You got ya' penis out ready to fuck me like I'm just some hoe off the street and I'm not" I challenged. He looked frustrated.

"Man alright, we'll wait to do it another time." He put his penis back in his pants, adjusted his pants and walked off back to his room.

Damn, you can't even wait for me to get myself together first? I thought. Once I fixed myself up, I walked back to the room and everyone was laughing.

"What's so funny? What I miss?" I asked.

"We're laughing at BJ dumbass; he's always saying some stupid shit." Ashley replied smiling and playfully slapping BJ's arm.

Hmmm, I wonder what they were doing, I thought.

"Alright man, y'all ready to go?" Tyrek asked. I rolled my eyes.

"Yeah, I'm ready to go to" I huffed. Ashley and BJ looked at us sideways. BJ smirked,

"Why y'all ready to go so soon?" he questioned. I tried to hide my anger because facial expressions always gave away my true feelings. I hated that.

"Nothing, I'm just tired plus Ashley need to get back home

before she gets in trouble" I mumbled.

"Alright, fuck it then. Let's roll out" BJ spoke.

Ashley and I walked ahead so we could talk. Ashley kept smiling. "I'm so happy to be see you, I love being around here so much."

Yea, I 'm glad too" I said.

"BJ told me I talk white, I feel like a lame" she blurted. "Girl the way you talk don't make you lame. Everybody got different accents. Ain't nun' wrong with speaking proper English. Don't let nobody make you feel like you gotta' mess up on words n' shit just to fit in with them. That's dumb" I went on.

She laughed, "I know. I really like BJ though."

"Really? What were y'all doing anyway? I see you ain't stopped smiling since we got off the train" I informed.

"Don't judge me" she spluttered.

"Girl, I ain't gone judge you, I ain't even like that" I retorted.

"Okay, I let him finger me because I'm still a virgin" she confessed. I stopped dead in my tracks.

"Wait, really?!" I asked surprised.

"Yeah." He wanted to have sex too, but I didn't want to."

" Bitch, you bold to even let that happen since you're a virgin" I giggled.

"I was nervous" she gushed.

I couldn't hide the shock from my face.

"Please don't tell nobody Jasmine!"

"I won't. We're cousins, you know I got you." I dropped the topic and we continued walking to the bus stop on 51st to head back to the East side.

BJ and Ashley were back boo'd up once we got on the bus. On the other hand, me and Tyrek rode in silence the entire ride and I hated it.

Once off the bus, we walked in silence down the block to Mary's house. We stopped a few houses down for Ashley and BJ to say their final goodbyes. "BJ, hurry up. It's cold as fuck out here'!" Tyrek yelled shaking.

"Nigga, shut up. Don't rush me. You shakin' like a stripper, tighten up." BJ boasted laughing, Tyrek didn't find it funny.

"That shit ain't funny, just hurry up" Tyrek annoyed.

"Yeah, whatever" BJ dismissed. Ashley hugged BJ and they became engrossed in passionate kissing for what seemed like eternity.

"Alright nigga, you gone see her again. I'm ready to go, nigga I'm freezing!" I'm glad Tyrek interrupted because it was awkward between us. I didn't wanna look like a cockblocker. They finally let go of each other and I walked Ashley up to the house. We barely knocked on the door before it swung open.

"I said to have her back by 10 PM, it's well after midnight!" Miss Mary screamed. She caught me off guard. I didn't expect for her to scream at us even though she was mad. I stayed quiet for a while thinking Ashley would give her a reason why she was late. "Well, I'm listening!"

She was only glaring at me but never looked at Ashley. I looked at Ashley and she never said anything, just stood with her head down. I stumbled getting my words out. "We umm--"

"We nothing! Don't expect for her to go anywhere else with you" she rasped. I glared at her. I finally mustered up enough courage to say okay and started walking down the pathway back to the street. I waved my hand slightly.

"Bye Ashley."

"Bye" she replied. I heard Mary tell her to come in the house in the distance. By the time I got back down the block to BJ and Tyrek my demeanor had completely changed.

"Alright, where we 'bout to go?" I asked.

"Man, I'm tired. I'm going back to the crib" Tyrek said.

"What time is it?" I asked. BJ looked at his phone,

"It's 1:45 AM, fuck it. Ima stay at yo' crib tonight bro'."

"Alright. Jas where you about to go?" Tyrek asked.

"It's too late to go back to Amber house. They might not answer the door and I don't wanna be out this late by myself. Can y'all take the bus with be back there to see if anybody answers?" I asked. They got quiet and just looked at each other.

"Jas, it's cold as hell and I'm sleepy" BJ said.

"Okay, the only other option is for me to spend a night at Tyrek house with y'all tonight and leave in the morning. Tyrek is that cool with you?" I questioned.

"Shit, I ain't trippin.' Let's just go because I'm cold as hell." Once we got back to Tyrek house it was well after 2AM and it had begun snowing. We walked inside the house and BJ went to the living room and plopped down on the couch while I followed Tyrek back to his room. He was on the phone with some random bitch selling her a dream, talking about how they were gonna get married.

I walked in the room with Tyrek and immediately asked for something to sleep in. He tossed me some basketball shorts and a wife beater. I changed clothes and slid in the bed under the blanket. I laid down, wrapped up in the blanket and waited until Tyrek got in the bed with me. Once the lights were turned off and the door was closed, he laid down, put his arms around me, and pulled me close. I felt relaxed and safe, something I hadn't felt in months. As I laid cuddled up in his arms, I drifted off to sleep.

Feeling aroused, I thought I was dreaming. My eyes were still closed, and I wasn't fully woke. I felt Tyrek's hands tugging at my shorts trying to untie them. I continued to fake like I was asleep and let him work to get my shorts untied. I felt his fingers run down my pussy and rub my clit. While his hands explored my pussy, I kept my eyes closed.

One finger entered, two fingers... I let out a small moan but kept my eyes closed. I couldn't help it, the shit felt good.

I hope he replaces his fingers with his tongue, I thought.

I wanted him in the worst way, but I was also beyond tired. *Maybe he'll see that I'm sleepy and will eventually stop.* Although I wanted him, I just didn't have enough energy to engage in any physical sex acts beyond him exploring my pussy with his tongue.

He began tugging at my shorts struggling to get them off. He continuously tried to pull them down, I slightly lifted my ass to make it easier for him. Excited, I anticipated his tongue meeting my sex. Instead, I was greeted with his rough fingers jamming inside of me. He was so rough that I became turned off. What was once moist and waiting for him was now dry and I was hoping he would stop.

I waited for him to finish so I could turn over and go to sleep. He continued plummeting my pussy with his rough fingers, he even had the nerve to try to stick in a third finger, but I stopped him. As soon as I stopped him, he slid his fingers out and I took my chance. I turned over swiftly before he could try to stop me.

I thought I was safe until I felt his rough hands pulling my shoulder to make me turnover. He succeeded and immediately whipped his penis out in front of my face.

"Suck my dick" he demanded.

I quickly sat up in the bed, my head tilted to the side with a typical black girl attitude to match.

"Excuse me!? You couldn't ask me nicer than that? You got me fucked up nigga'!"

He made a little sad puppy dog face, it was kind of cute, but I couldn't let him know that.

"Man, my bad. Can I get some head though?" he whined.

"Nigga that ain't much better but whatever" I snapped.

"Come on baby, please? You gone let me get blue balls?" He stood up in front of me looking sad, while stroking his manhood to life. I started pouting. My lips poked out, with the saddest puppy dog eyes.

"Baby I'm tired, I don't feel like it" I whined.

"Please baby?" he pleaded.

"No, I'm tired" I retorted.

"Alright bitch, you owe me a favor. I'm letting you stay here because yo' ass ain't got nowhere to go. So, what you gone do for me?" I just stared at him with a blank look.

"If you can't do nun' for me then maybe you don't need to be here" he sneered.

Was he kicking me out his house?

I was shocked, I looked up at him and gone was the sad puppy dog eyes and innocent look. Staring at me was a man with a menacing look that showed me he meant business. I weighed my options. I could leave but where would I go? If I did go somewhere, how would I explain to them why I was running the streets at almost 4AM? Where would I stay warm at?

Shit, why does it have to be snowing outside right now? I thought.

"Tyrek can I just go to sleep for at least an hour or two then wake up and do this?" I begged.

"No, do it right now! I ain't gone be in the mood later. You don't even gotta give me head for a long time. Just get it wet enough so I can stick it in yo' pussy" he suggested.

"Tyrek, I don't feel like fucking you. I can make you horny again later. Just chill."

I proceeded to lay down and was pulled back up by my hair. Tyrek had my hair bawled up in his fist and had snatched me back up. He snatched me up wildly and I came face to face with his penis again. He put his penis on my lips, rubbing his manhood across them and attempted to push his penis in my mouth but I refused to open.

"Bitch stop playing with me! Suck my dick before I put yo' ass out with no clothes on." He snarled.

I slowly opened my mouth and he quickly jammed his penis in and began fast stroking in and out of my mouth. Tyrek was still holding my hair, so I didn't bother to try to move. I just stayed still while he pumped in and out of my mouth. He jerked my head away from his penis.

"Suck my dick like you want to before I throw you outside butt ass naked in the cold" he repeated.

I wanted to cry so bad, but I couldn't show him I was weak because he would only take advantage of that. I slowly moved over so I could give him room to lay down.

"Come lay down" I quavered.

He laid down and I immediately took his penis in my hands and slowly stroked it back to life. I examined his penis, it was long and skinny, so I figured it wouldn't be that bad. I licked the tip then slowly put my mouth over the tip of his penis and started licking the shaft of his penis up and down.

After about five minutes of sucking his penis I was tired. Every time I tried to stop; he wouldn't let me. He would only push my head down further and have me choking on his penis. I tried to make him cum but every time I was close, I would stop or slow down. He blamed me, but my jaws were starting to lock.

I pulled out all my best tricks to make him cum quicker. I looked him dead in the eye seductively while I sucked him up, I even sucked on his balls at the same time. With my left hand, I was giving him a hand job, while giving him a blowjob, while I played with my pussy with my right hand. He tried to be gentle when he seen my eyes were red and watery from him constantly making me gag by pushing my head down and holding it there, but he still didn't let me stop.

"Baby take your time, don't throw up on my penis" he expressed. I cringed, I wanted so badly to be alone. I felt violated.

"What the fuck?!" I immediately popped Tyrek's penis out of my mouth and pulled my head back before he could push it back into mouth. BJ burst in the room laughing with a mischievous grin on his face. "Damn, y'all in this motherfucker' getting it in."

I screamed out in pain to Tyrek yanking me by my hair. "What the fuck you do that for?" I yelled. Did I tell yo' ass to stop? Now you see how I feel. You scraped my penis with yo' teeth tryna' get up!" he shouted.

"Sorry!" I exclaimed. Tyrek was starting to look more and more intimidating to me. I quickly threw the blanket over my body. Tyrek laughed, "Damn bro, yo' ass can't knock?"

"Nigga' we brothers', ion' knock on doors. I damn near live here too" he shrugged.

"Yea, you right" Tyrek agreed.

"Um, can you get out BJ?" I asked.

"Why I gotta get out? Y'all can do what y'all was doing, I ain't gone bother y'all." I watched BJ sit down in a nearby chair. I was embarrassed.

"Tyrek, baby can you please tell him to get out?" He

chuckled. "Tyrek, I'm serious!"

"Aye bro, get out' he stated nonchalantly.

"No, why I gotta get out? This is my room too; I sleep right here on the floor" he joked.

I rolled my eyes, "You're so annoying" I stated.

"Bro get out."

"No y'all can finish. Just act like I ain't here" he giggled.

"Bro', you doing too much. You not gone let me get my nut off real' quick? I'm not about to fuck while you in here so you can see my penis. Nigga' that's gay" he stated.

"Bro, I ain't gay either. Ion' wanna see yo' penis. Let me hit after you." BJ suggested. My eyes damn near popped out of my head.

"BJ, you're like a brother to me. Why would you even think of me that way? You not bout' to hit shit up over here!" I shrieked. Tyrek laughed.

"What the fuck you laughing at? You not gone take up for me or anything?" I groaned.

"Aye, I ain't gone nun' to do with that. If you wanna let bros' hit, then that's up to you" he mocked.

"You know I don't want that! I'm not a hoe! I'm only doing this with you because I really like you" I stated. They both burst out laughing and my feelings were seriously hurt.

"Alright bro' get out so I can bust this nut really quick."

"Bro, I'm not leaving so you better figure out something" BJ insisted. Tyrek looked at me and said "Fuck it. Come finish sucking my penis. You weren't supposed to stop anyway" he snapped.

"Tyrek I'm not bout' to do anything with somebody else in the room watching us!"

"Man shut the fuck up" Tyrek said. I didn't even have enough time to protest before I was yanked by my hair and pulled down face to face with his penis. I pulled the covers over my head and said a silent prayer.

Lord please let this be over quick. Please let this stop God. A tear escaped down my cheek, but I quickly wiped it away.

The entire time I was praying, Tyrek he was showing off. He was pushing my head down harder and saying shit like "Yea suck that shit" and "Ima make you swallow my kids." I felt so disgusted. Smacked with cold air, the blanket was snatched from me by BJ.

"Yeah, glad you did that bros. I need to see my penis fucking yo' mouth" Tyrek stated. I glanced up at BJ and noticed he had his phone in his hand. I looked back down and tried to focus on Tyrek's penis, which reminded me of a pencil because it was long and skinny. Pushing my head back, Tyrek told me to lay down, so he could "Fuck my brains out." I was so annoyed. Every nigga I encountered here was turning into a cornball. I laid down and allowed him to enter me missionary style, but my focus wasn't on him, it was on BJ. Something was weird about how he was holding his phone and looking at me.

Fake moaning, pretending like Tyrek was rocking my world, I studied BJ in the corner of the room. Tyrek's sex was good, but I couldn't fully enjoy it because how much of an asshole he had been to me. That alone, could make you lose interest in someone no matter how great the penis is. BJ was standing in the corner, leaning against the wall with his phone in hand that looked like it was pointed at me. My mind started to wonder, *is he recording us?* Fuck it, I'll ask him.

"Wait Tyrek hold on." He kept trying to stroke, he just slowed down.

"BJ, you recording us? I tried to say it jokingly, so Tyrek wouldn't try to punish me for it.

"I ain't recording y'all Jas. I'm just on my phone, on Facebook."

"Jas, that's what you tried to stop me for? Fuck him, that shit don't matter."

Tyrek began thrusting harder which made me get temporary amnesia. By the end of the night, Tyrek had put a hurtin' on me. He had hit it from the back and had me screaming his name. He had me wanting to cry, kill him, and love him all at the same time after that sex. I was unsure about Tyrek after that, I started thinking he was bipolar.

Tyrek cuddled up with me after that. BJ's ignorant ass wouldn't even let us put clothes on. After that rollercoaster sex, he refused to leave the room to even let us get dressed. We slept in the bed naked that night while BJ slept on the floor on a pallet.

CHAPTER FIVE

Playing for Keeps

W hat the fuck Tyrek!? I told you about bringing all these fast ass females in my house. Yo' ass need to get up, so you can be on time for work. You know you have to work today. It's 8 AM, you got an hour and a half to get up and be outta' here. Lil girl, whoever you are, you need to get up and go home" the unknown lady shrieked.

My heart was beating so fast, me and Tyrek were naked under the blankets and I hoped she didn't pull the blankets back.

"Tyrek, I said get up now!" she yelled.

"Alright ma, I'm about to get up."

This was his mom? This has gotta be the worst way to meet someone's mom, so much for first impression.

She stood at the door looking at us and I wondered if she was ever gonna leave for us to put on our clothes. I wanted to run out of there so bad. His mom finally walked away however she didn't bother closing the door. By then, BJ had woken up and was already on his phone. "Alright bro, get out really quick so we can get dressed."

"Alright" BJ stated. Tyrek pushed the door closed after he left, and we got dressed. I didn't wanna walk back in Amber's house with the same clothes on. That just screamed hoe behavior.

"Tyrek can I get some clothes to put on just to get home?" He threw me a navy blue Southern high school sweatshirt and a pair of grey sweatpants. "You go to Southern?"

"Yeah."

"I know people that go to Southern" I stated.

"Aw yeah? That's wassup" he replied. I felt so stupid. *Of course, he goes to Southern.* He was living in my old neighborhood. There was only a few select schools you could possibly be going to if you lived around this area. He either went to Wilburg, Brownsville, Hyde Park, Dyer, Southern, or King. I knew damn near everyone at all of those schools, so it was a "lose-lose" situation for me. It didn't matter because we more than likely were all from the same neighborhood if we went to these schools and knew the same people.

I was dressed within five minutes and was ready to be out the door. I sat on a nearby chair in the room and waited for Tyrek to finish getting dressed. "Are you gone walk me to the bus stop?"

"Yeah, let's go" he responded. We were almost out the door when he told me to hold on, so he could get his headphones.

Shit, I hope his mom doesn't come out here and see me again. I waited by the front door, nervously shaking my leg. "Sweetheart, what's yo' name?" Tyrek's mom asked once she walked out of the kitchen and ran right into me. I wanted to disappear so bad.

"Umm Jasmine."

"Jasmine, you said?" she questioned.

"Yes" I stated biting my fingers, I was nervous about what she was about to say to me.

"My name is Toni, listen here, don't let these boys take advantage of you and use you like you're nothing out here. That's my son and I'm telling you don't let my son take advantage of you and disrespect you. You're a pretty girl, respect yourself." I quickly wiped away a tear that escaped down my cheek.

"Okay, I'm sorry for disrespecting your---."

"Alright, you ready? Let's go" Tyrek interrupted. Tyrek had walked out the door and was rushing me out of the apartment. He was giving me a puzzled angry look. I assumed he didn't want me talking to his mother.

"Alright, nice to meet you sweetheart and remember what I said" Toni said. Tyrek immediately put his headphones on and walked ahead of me. I slowed down even more just to see if he would notice and wait for me.

"Why you walking so slow?" he turned around and asked.

"Boy don't rush me. You see it's a lot of snow out here" I scoffed. We got to the bus stop and waited for the bus for about ten minutes. I used that as an opportunity to see how he felt about me. Although I was upset about the events the night before, I foolishly still liked him.

"So, am I gone' hear from you any time after today?" I questioned.

"Shit, I don't know. You can hit me up" he suggested.

"Why do I have to hit you up? You not gone check on me or nothing?" I asked

"Man, you trippin' he fumed.

"Yea, I'm always trippin' when it's something a motherfucker don't wanna hear." I countered.

"Jas, stop trippin,' Ima' hit you up alright?" he assured.

"Mhm, we'll see."

"Come here Jas" he said.

I mean mugged him, I wanted to be mad at him so bad, but I also wanted to be wrapped up in his arms. He was so damn fine. He had on some all-white air force ones, some grey sweatpants, a black North Face jacket, an all-black skully hat, and some black gloves.

"Jas stop playing with me. Come here man!" I slowly walked

over to him, pretending to be mad. He yanked me close to his body once I got within arm's reach. He pulled me close, "Jas, you better stop playing with me." He looked into my eyes and I quickly looked away. I hated for people to look me in my eyes.

He turned my head back towards him and kissed me. We stood hugged up and kissing for the next two minutes. I gave him one last peck kiss and told him I was gone' miss him. We cuddled up at the bus stop for the rest of the wait until the bus came.

When the bus came, I didn't want to get on. If he didn't have to go to work and his mom wasn't home, I would've ditched the bus and stayed with him. I felt stupid for wanting to be around him after everything he did to me last night, but I couldn't help it. He gave me a hug and a kiss and walked off while I boarded the bus. I watched him walk back towards the house while other passengers boarded the bus. It took me about 30 minutes to get back to Amber's house. I made it back to Amber's house around 9:15 AM. I walked in and immediately went to Amber's room.

I didn't say anything to anyone because I didn't want them asking me questions about where I'd been. I walked in Amber's room and she was sitting up flicking through the TV. "Hey" I greeted her. Amber was looking at me weird.

"Hey" she said. She looked me up and down and continued flicking through the TV channels. I took off my jackets and went to plug up my government phone. "Where were you at last night?" she asked.

"Oh, I went down to my old friend 's house on the low end, I stayed with her for the night because it was late by the time we left from downtown."

"Yo' friend go to Southern?"

"No, but she used to."

"That looks like Tyrek's sweatshirt" she stated.

Fuck, how does she know that?

"How does this look like his shirt? It's a thousand other kids that could have these sweatshirts, anybody that go to that school."

"I remember you telling me before you came up here that you ain't really fuck with none of them on 35th no more. Also, Tyrek's on the basketball team and that sweatshirt says 'Southern basketball on it. You spent a night with Tyrek?" she asked smirking.

"Gee, you trippin' don't nobody want ya' nigga. Even if I did spend the night with him, why does it matter? You don't even fuck with him, he told me y'all don't even talk. But like I said, I don't fuck with him."

"Yeah alright, if you say so." I tried to look like I was unbothered by the conversation and she was trippin' but in my mind, I was going crazy. How could I be so stupid?

I need to get out of this house, this "friendship" won't be lasting long. I thought.

"Can I sleep in yo' bed?" I asked.

"What's wrong with the floor?" she replied snidely.

I smacked my lips, "you're acting like you're jealous of me, never mind me asking."

"No, I ain't jealous, I just feel like being in my own bed" she snarled.

"I guess" I sighed. I grabbed a blanket out of the closet, made a pallet on the floor and went back to sleep. I was beyond exhausted.

I woke up at two PM, took a shower and I was out of there within an hour and a half. Amber and Marcus weren't there when I left. I called my auntie Yvonne and told her I was in Chicago. She was a little upset at me, and I already knew she was about to scold me, but I was starting to miss my real family. I needed to be around somebody that I shared the same bloodline with. I was happy because I didn't want to see Marcus and I didn't want Amber to figure out anything that happened with us.

My auntie sent my big cousin Nashay to come get me. Now Nashay was bad as fuck. She was tall, had a flat tummy, and a coke bottle shape. My cousin had all the niggas wanting her, I wanted a shape like hers, it was even better that she was pretty and always stayed fly. Many said she resembled a younger version of Taraji P Henson. I always felt she should model.

Part of me wanted to go to my auntie's house because I was

hoping she would feel bad for me and take me shopping or give me some clothes, at least a coat. I was freezing! I still had the money my uncle gave me, but I hadn't made it to the mall.

"Yo' ass really rode a damn bus all the way to Chicago?!" My cousin and I had just walked in the house and my auntie were already starting to grill me about my latest bullshit. I expected that. I gave my auntie a hug,

"I had to get away from everything that was going on. My daddy is really abusive and he's an alcoholic."

"Baby trust me, I know ya' daddy an alcoholic. Yo' daddy takes a drink before he even washes his ass in the morning. That's a damn shame" she grumbled.

I plopped down on the bed, "Y'all got something to eat?" I asked.

"Yeah, go in that kitchen and look for something to eat" my aunt stated. I found some pizza puffs in the deep freezer and asked Nashay to cook them for me.

"Girl you don't know how to cook?" she questioned.

"Not really, I don't want to burn it and waste food." After Nashay made my food, Auntie Yvonne called me back in her room. "Come in here, we need to talk, let me know everything that's been going on." I started telling her about the first time my daddy hit me, and I realized he was abusive. Not only physically, but mentally as well.

We had been talking for about three hours. The conversation

was full of sadness and depression, but it had some funny moments. Auntie Yvonne called my mom and they talked for about an hour while Nashay and I listened. I heard my auntie tell my mom she wanted to get me a coat because I could possibly catch pneumonia.

My auntie had money; she was one of the most successful people in my family. She drove a Benz, her kids stayed fly, and she worked downtown as a court clerk. Although she had become legally successful, it was just a front to cover her reality. She was still deep in the streets. She dated the biggest drug dealer in the Chicago area.

She even helped females obtain benefits even when they didn't qualify in return for them to boost clothes and shoes. She was the hood fairy godmother. Around 7PM, Nashay asked me if I wanted to go with her to her friend's house, she only lived across the street. I went with her because I didn't want to be stuck in the house with my auntie. Besides, Nashay was only two years older than me. I had more in common with her than my auntie.

"What's up bitch?" Nashay walked in her friend house and laid on the couch. I was uncomfortable, but I was trying not to make it noticeable. While we were waiting for her friend to come downstairs, we heard her hollering at her kids. I was curious if she was the same age as Nashay because Nashay was only eighteen, going on nineteen. Nashay's friend finally came downstairs.

"Resha, this is my lil' cousin Jas and Jas this is Resha."

I smiled, "Hey." Resha said hey back, after that Nashay and Resha acted like I wasn't even there. I was low-key pissed and ready to get back to the city. I knew I was a little younger, but they could've at least tried to include me in the conversation. I felt they didn't want me there and I was ready to go.

After about an hour, Nashay got up and said, "We're about to go home." We went back across the street and my auntie asked me where I was about to go. I told her they could take me back where they picked me up from. Now I had an attitude. I figured if she was asking me where I was about to go, and it was only 8 o' clock she was giving me a hint that I couldn't stay there.

"Nashay, take her back to wherever you picked her up from" my aunt stated.

"Alright, I'll take her because I have to go to that neighborhood anyway" Nashay replied.

We got ready to walk out the door and my auntie grabbed me. "You be safe out here and call me if you need me for anything" she proclaimed.

I smirked, "Alright." *You ain't gone help me with shit. You can clearly see I only have on two thin ass jackets. I'm staying with random ass people, to be honest,* I thought.

Once we got in the car, Nashay started blasting Future's song, *'Same Damn Time.'* " I have to pick up my friend in Calumet City first, okay?"

"Okay, can we stop at Sharks since we're going that way?"

"Yeah."

80

Sharks was a corner restaurant in Chicago and the food was simply heaven! They were famous for their lemon pepper chicken, butter cookies, and their gizzards. Now, I ain't eat Gizzards but my grandma loved them! My auntie lived in Chicago Heights, which was right outside of Chicago. Don't get the wrong impression, the suburbs in Illinois were no better than the actual city of Chicago. Well, it depended on what suburbs you were referring to. There was still just as many killings and gang related activities. In fact, most of the people living in the suburbs were originally from the city and they didn't make it any better.

After I retrieved my food, we headed to Nashay's friend house. We pulled up in front of a run-down apartment building and Jaliah walked out. I got excited,

"I didn't know you were coming to get Jaliah!" I knew Jaliah, I had met her at one of our family gatherings a few years back. She'd been like my big sister from that day. She always had my back, looked out for me, and included me in everything they did. She was the only one out of Nashay's friends that I really liked and always excited to see. I got in the back seat and let Jaliah sit in the front.

"Hey Jas, I missed you!" I blushed and said "Hey" while trying to keep my composure. I became mad at myself, I hated when I did that. After we stopped to get my food, the rest of the ride was turnt'. Jaliah cracked jokes the rest of the way. I couldn't wait until I was their age and had my own car. We pulled up to Amber's house and I didn't want to get out of the car. I prolonged getting out the car because I didn't feel like being bothered with any of Amber's family.

"Nashay, can you come and get me another one of these days?" I asked.

"Yeah, just text me or call my mom and I'll come get you" she agreed.

"Alright, see y'all later."

"Bye Jas, see you later" Jaliah said. I dreaded walking into Amber's house. I was slowly getting fed up with staying there.

CHAPTER SIX

Turn of Events

The tension was thick as soon as I walked in the house. It was unusually quiet. Amber was in her room watching TV and Marcus was on the computer as usual. If he wasn't smoking, or on the block somewhere then he was on Facebook, flexing. I walked in Amber's room to put my things up and walked back out. We barely exchanged words beside a simple "Hey."

I walked back in the living room, sat down, and watched TV. From the corner of my eye, I noticed Marcus staring at me. Every time I would make eye contact with him, he would look away. I eventually ignored his clear attempts to get my attention. He got tired of me ignoring him and came to sit by me on the couch. He sat so close to me that we were touching.

"Damn, can I get some room? You're in my personal space" I uttered.

"Jas, you trippin.' I'm comfortable, you move then since you need yo' personal space." I moved over a few inches and he was all over me. As soon as I moved, he immediately followed me. I rolled my eyes and continued watching television like he wasn't there despite his obvious attempts to get my attention. I slowly drifted off to sleep.

I woke up to nudging me awake. "Wake up Jas" he urged as he left a trail of kisses from my neck down to my chest.

He lifted up, grabbed my face, and kissed me passionately. He unzipped his pants and let his penis free. He looked at me seductively while stroking his manhood. "Take these off" he ordered while tapping me on shorts. "No, I can't. I started my period this morning" I lied. I was still a bit annoyed about our last encounter.

"How about you give me some head?" he asked. He looked nervous. I immediately became annoyed and couldn't hide it on my face.

I ignored him, pushed him off me and hauled ass down the hallway back to Amber's room. I ran right into Nima coming out of her room. "Damn Nima, I thought y'all were sleep" I spluttered.

"No, we're just watching television. What you doing still up?" she asked.

"Aw, I'm about to go to bed now. I had to use the bathroom" I lied.

"Oh, someone's in the bathroom in the front? she questioned. "I didn't see anyone in there." I tried my best not to look guilty.

"Shit, I don't know if they're in there now, but someone was in there earlier" I said.

"Aw, it must've been Marcus" she said.

"Yeah, it probably was" I replied.

"Alright, I'm about to go to bed. Goodnight" she said.

"Goodnight."

Thank God she hadn't seen Marcus, I thought. I walked in Amber's room to get some pajamas out of my suitcase. I walked to the front to the bathroom to take a quick shower. I showered, got dressed, grabbed a blanket and laid on Amber's floor. I got as comfortable as I could on the hardwood floor then realized I hadn't used the bathroom before I took a shower.

Damn, I really don't feel like getting up. I reluctantly got up to use the bathroom.

As soon as I was out of the bathroom, walking back to Amber's room I ran into Marcus. I tried to walk past him like he wasn't there, but he grabbed me by my waist and pulled me close. I didn't bother resisting him because I wanted it. I didn't want sex from him, but he had a way of making me feel loved, even if I knew it wasn't real love. He kissed me and slapped me on the ass.

"Take yo' ass to bed" he said.

I laughed, "That's what I was trying to do before you stopped me" I commented.

"Damn, bitch where you at? I'm freezing."

I was standing at the bus stop on King Drive waiting for Meka.

"Girl, I'm about to get off the bus right now" she answered.

I was waiting for her so we could go to Ford City Mall. When I was young that mall used to be the spot, lately I was hearing that it wasn't poppin' anymore but whatever, I still wanted to go. It was New Year's Eve, and we were going to find a nice fit to wear to the Gutta Boys party they were throwing on the Northside.

We had to be fly because their parties were always turnt' up and their crew was full of fine ass niggas with money. I had called Meka three times in the past twenty minutes and each time she kept saying she was only "A few minutes away."

Black people can never be on time, I sighed.

I finally saw her get off the bus and we ran across the street to catch the bus all the way to the mall. "Gee, you wanna' go to Golden Corral while we're up here?" Meka asked.

"Hell yeah, I could eat!" I exclaimed.

During the long bus ride, we talked about our plans for the night. We planned to "Pre-game" at Meka's house then head to the

Gutta Boys party at eleven. I just needed a few drinks before we headed out so I could relax.

I used to be a part of another clique, like Gutta Boys, before I moved to Dallas, but I left that alone. Gang banging, fighting, and throwing parties was not something I wanted to do. In Chicago, most of us would be lucky to even make it to see eighteen. I loved my life, even if shit was fucked up.

After shopping, I didn't feel like sitting somewhere to eat and it was already getting late.

"Let's go back to the hood and slide to the corner restaurant." Meka was cool with it so we hopped back on the city bus and rode back to her house.

By the time we got near the train station, it was packed. The bus was turnt! It was filled with fine niggas and ratchet ghetto bitches with long weaves and pea coats. There wasn't any violence; the vibe was great. Times like this made me love Chicago so much. It was dark by the time we were almost home so Meka called a boy she was fucking with from around the way, Isaiah, and had him meet us at the bus stop.

We got off the bus and we didn't see Isaiah anywhere. "This nigga got me fucked up, hold up, I'm about to call him."

She called him and didn't get an answer, so we started walking to the corner restaurant to get us some food before we got to the house.

We were alert because in Chicago you always had to watch

yo' back and yo' surroundings. Right before we crossed the train tracks, Isaiah, and his niggas ran out of the alley acting like they had guns. We bolted running then we realized it was their stupid asses playing! "Y'all play too fucking much, you almost made me drop my bags!" Meka yelled hitting Isaiah in the chest.

"Y'all almost gave me a fucking heart attack" I heaved.

"You'll be alright, lil' gee. Don't get caught lackin'" Isaiah reminded laughing. He might've been laughing but I knew he was serious about his statement.

When we finally got to the corner restaurant, Meka and I ordered our food while Isaiah made beats on the table. Some other nigga I didn't know started rhyming.

"Alright, fuck it up then!" I started laughing and hyping it up while Meka started dancing.

We were turnt' until the old Arab started banging on the bullet proof glass threatening to kick us out and call the police. We got our food and walked back to Meka's house.

"Meka we gotta hurry up and eat our food so we can get dressed and bitch, don't forget you need to do my hair" I reminded her once we walked in her house.

"It's better if Rakia does it, she's better at doing hair than me and she can make yo' bun bigger. You still tryna' get a bun with bangs in the front, right?" Meka asked.

"Yeah, I don't wanna' wear my hair down and sweat it out."

Rakia came downstairs and said she would do my hair, but I needed to hurry up, so she could get dressed too.

"Meka give me some towels so I can hop in the shower" I demanded.

"Look in the closet right there in the hallway, but don't use none of my momma good towels because you know she gone' trip on us!"

I laughed because everyone knew what "good towels" were. Those were the towels that were only for show and we were expected to know not to use 'em or we were getting our ass beat.

"Jas! Yo' "Obama" ringing!" Meka's little sister, Auri, yelled brining my phone to me. It was my mom calling me. I really missed her and part of me was feeling guilty for even leaving her. I had to snap out of it though because as a mother, she shouldn't have even let me go through those beatings or emotional hurt. Shit, she shouldn't have even let it happen to her, I felt like my mom was weak and I hated that about her.

"Hey ma!"

"What are you doing?" she questioned.

"Nothing, at my friend house. How's everybody doing? You

going to church tonight?" I asked.

My momma got quiet for a while. "Yeah, we're going to church tonight, the same place you need to be at, and I know that's not where you're going tonight. Am I right?"

"I'm going to a little celebration at my friend house" I stated.

"So, you're going to a party. Look, you're not grown and running away to an entirely different state was wrong. Your dad does have his problems, but he hasn't done anything that extreme for you to do all of this. I'm booking your ticket back home; I'm not going to let you stay with your grandmother. She's too old to be stressed about trying to take care of a teenager. You are not grown! Don't even think about trying to hide at one of yo' lil friend's house or miss yo' flight because I will be on the next flight out to come get you!" she ranted.

"Mom really?" I questioned. The other day you were all for me, saying I wasn't wrong, and you were just glad I was safe. You're gonna make me come back somewhere that ain't safe for me or you!? You never stand up to daddy whenever he does anything to you, me or Minnie. Mom, when are you gonna start sticking up for yourself!? That's why Minnie left because she said you changed! You never let people run over you and you act like you're scared of that man!" I countered.

"That man is your father and I am not scared of your dad! You're coming home, you're not about to stay in Chicago so you can run the streets with no supervision. End of discussion." She objected.

I became silent because I was debating if I should curse her ass out, but I decided against that because I didn't know what type of shit she would pull. I had to play this smart.

"Alright, bye."

I hung up the phone, sat on the edge of the tub while I waited for the water to warm up. Before I knew it, I was crying. *God, why are you allowing me to go through this? Haven't I been through enough?* I thought.

I had to get myself together. Fuck it, I was going home in a few days, so I figured I might as well turn up and have fun for the remainder of my time. I knew going back to Dallas meant going back to prison. My time in Chicago was equivalent to the time you have free to enjoy your last moments before being sentenced to prison.

I showered, got dressed, and waited for Rakia to finish getting dressed so she could do my hair. A feeling of sadness took over me. Meka walked in the room. "What's wrong with you? Your eyes are red.

"Nothing, I think I'm a little sleepy, I'll be alright though" I dismissed.

"You can't be going to sleep girl; you better eat and throw some water in ya' face" she piped.

"Gee you look cute!" she complimented.

"Thank you Meka."

"You think this look right on me?" Meka asked.

She sported all blacking leggings, a red tank top, and a baseball jersey over it.

"Yes girl, you look cute" I said.

"Gee I think I'll be freezing" she mumbled.

"Gee you good, we're gonna be in the house, once you start dancing and drinking, you're gonna be hot" I assured her.

I had on black leggings, a shimmery blue and black loose-fitting tank top that had 'Hot Girl' plastered in neon green letters, with some black boots that resembled Ugg's, but they were knock offs. Lord knows, I certainly couldn't afford the real thing. My outfit was cute, but we had to walk to the party. I knew that cold air was gone' smack me in the face as soon as I stepped outside.

"Jas C'mon so I can do your hair" Rakia called.

"Alright."

After Rakia did my hair, I was feeling myself. I grabbed Meka's camera and snapped pics of myself for about the next thirty minutes.

"Dam gee, how many pics you gone' take?" Meka questioned.

"Girl you know I gotta' find the right one. Ima' take about fifty and delete about forty-seven of 'em."

Meka laughed, "Gee you crazy."

"Y'all just gone' leave us like that? It's alright, we gone have more fun than y'all anyway. We 'bout to turn up!" Meka's aunt boasted as she walked in the room with a cup of Patron in her hand. "Y'all want some? There's some more downstairs."

"I want some but not too much, I'm trying to drink at the party too" I explained.

Auri and I went downstairs and started pouring cups. By the time everyone else were finished getting dressed, I was on my third bottle of Green Apple Smirnoff.

"Y'all ass down here throwing shots back to back." Rakia said.

"Y'all ready to go?" Meka asked.

"Yeah, let's go" I chimed in.

Meka hollered upstairs to tell everyone we were leaving. I reluctantly put on my two jackets. They didn't match with my outfit and I certainly was gonna freeze outside but I took my chances anyway. I just hoped the liquor I had been drinking helped keep my warm.

We walked outside looking like quadruplets by the head. We all sported buns in our hair with a side bang. We were fly. While walking down the street, Meka handed everyone a blade to stick under their tongue. Chicago was no place to walk at night without a weapon. Together, me, Rakia, Meka, and Mee-Mee walked five blocks over to the party. Mee-Mee was another one our homegirls from around the way. She lived in the same neighborhood with us.

We only seen her at school or riding passenger side down the block with some young dope dealer in the neighborhood. If it wasn't about money, she mostly stayed to herself. Tonight, was a special occasion since it was New Year's Eve.

CHAPTER SEVEN

Drunken Night

When we walked in the party, it was turnt! The DJ was playing all of the jams. They had open bar for everyone the entire night. We walked in took off our coats and went to get our first drinks. I didn't tell anyone, but today was my first time drinking so I was a little excited. I only knew alcohol made you warm because my dad often bragged about not having to wear a coat during the winter months while everyone else suffered in the cold weather. Although I'd lived with an alcoholic, I never once dared to taste any of his drinks. Meka pulled my hand through the crowd,

"Gee let's go get drinks." I followed Meka who ordered her drink, "What you want to drink?"

I tried to act nonchalant, "It don't matter. Whatever you get, I'm cool with." The bartender gave us large cups, I watched as she made our drinks. She poured mostly alcohol and put about 5% juice in the drink. I stared wide-eyed.

I don't know if I can drink that, I thought. The bartender handed me my drink and I hesitated to take it. I took my drink and went to sit with Meka and the rest of the girls.

We sat and observed the scene while niggas came and mingled with us here and there. They mostly came to talk to Mee-Mee. Mee-Mee was a bad ass female. She was young, but she didn't look her age, at only fifteen years old. She had full breasts, big hips, and an ass to match. With caramel skin and long straight blonde hair, she looked straight out of a music video. I wasn't mad though because if I was a nigga, I probably would've hollered at her too.

I looked at the girls and they were sipping on their drinks, so I decided to sip mine. The first taste caught me by surprise, it burned. My eyes got watery, I was tempted to throw the whole drink away, but I didn't want to look inexperienced. Mee-Mee was fifteen and was sipping her drink with no problems. I tried to take another swig and cringed.

Ugh, how can people drink this? What's so good about this at all? I thought. The drink I had now tasted totally different than the Smirnoff's I had downed earlier that night.

After an hour of taking tiny sips, I said fuck it. Jas, you got this I told myself. I took a deep breath, swallowed hard, threw my head back and guzzled the entire drink. Feeling like I had just burned a hole in my chest, I sat down and tried to recollect myself.

"Fuck! This shit burns!" I said.

I got up and looked for Meka because somewhere between

my drinking and sitting down she had vanished. I found her in the kitchen making herself a plate. "Damn gee, you ain't eat at home?" I asked.

"No, gee. But I'm about to smash this plate though."

"I see" I smirked.

She laughed, "Shit you talking about me eating but you done killed that drink!"

"Girl yea, I don't wanna' remember shit by the morning" I joked.

We both laughed.

"True, that's when you know you had the best night, I can't even finish mines though" Meka said.

"You can't? Shit, give it to me. I'll drink it" I urged.

"Gee, you gone be drunk as hell before it even hit twelve" she said laughing.

"Gee, if I am then I've accomplished my goal" I boasted.

We walked back in the party and for the next ten minutes, I sat and slowly downed the rest of my drink. I began feeling a lot more comfortable and I was feeling hot even though it was below zero degrees outside. I leaned over to Meka, "Gee you ain't hot?"

"Girl no, that's all that liquor you've been drinking" she explained.

I played it off, "Aw yeah, I forgot." I just nodded my head and smiled even though I didn't know the first thing there is to know when drinking which was don't mix drinks. I would soon find that out though. Mixing dark and light would leave you slumped.

Throughout the rest of the night, I mingled with everyone. I thought I was being friendly and starting to feel comfortable, but the females felt like I was being a hoe that needed to be dealt with. By eleven PM, I had also drank the rest of Mee-Mee's drink. I felt so comfortable; I was really feeling myself. I had plopped down on the couch next to some cute dark-skinned boy and was chatting him up. He was giving me his number when Meka walked up and sat next to me. "Aw hey Meka, this is um, damn I forgot his name." Meka ignored my remarks and leaned over to ask the guy his name.

"My name Chris" he stated.

"Okay, who you here with?" Meka asked.

"I'm here with Jalisa" he said.

"Jalisa with the red hair?" she questioned.

He said yeah. Meka grabbed my hand and pulled me up away from Chris.

"What are you doing? Why you pulling me?" I asked. Meka ignored me and continued to pull me through the crowd until we got to the bathroom. She shut the door and began scowling and disciplining me like I was her child.

"Gee, you need to get yo' shit together. You can't be out here just talking to anybody nigga. Most of these niggas in here came with their girl. Them bitches in there mugging you and if they keep doing it, we gone have problems and end up throwing hands. Don't talk to no niggas in here. This party too small for that" she ordered.

The liquor was taking over me because I couldn't even stand up straight, but I felt courageous. Leaning up against the sink, I snapped back.

"These bitches don't faze me, they just mad because they niggas want me. They ain't bold enough to step to me so I ain't worried."

"Gee, I know you ain't scared. Shit, I ain't either but I just don't wanna' get into it with them because we're all supposed to be family in this crew" she stressed.

"I got you, I ain't gone say shit as long as they don't say shit to me" I slurred.

"Alright, thank you. Don't be acting petty and shit because I know you girl." We both laughed.

"Girl I can't guarantee that because you know that's in my blood, but I'll try" I stated.

"Alright."

We walked out of the bathroom and I decided to chill for the rest of the night. I tried so hard to focus but I was starting to feel really dizzy, the room was spinning around me. The harder I tried to focus the less I felt in control of myself. I began shaking Meka roughly. "Meka I don't feel good. Damn, did somebody drug me?" Meka was busy rapping the lyrics to Chief Keef's hit song "*I Don't*

Like."

"Girl, what's wrong with you? You know nobody would drug you. You're just drunk, I mean you were finishing everyone's drink for them" she pointed out.

"Damn, you right. Let me just chill and maybe this feeling will go away."

"Yeah, just chill" Meka said. "I'll sit right here with you."

Feeling the urge to throw up, I quickly jumped up and tried to rush to the bathroom but didn't make it. Rushing to the bathroom, I tried covering my mouth because I felt the sensation coming. A pasty substance coated my mouth as it began watering. It felt as if a lever had been released to allow the fluids to flow as my stomach did flips. I had puked all over a man's arm that I didn't recognize. Rushing through the crowd, I faintly heard some ghetto ass girl screaming about her weave.

"Aw hell no! That bitch done threw up in my new weave! No, that bitch gotta go!" she screamed.

If I wasn't feeling like death was near, I would've gone back and said something, but I chose not to. I finally finished puking. Running water to clean myself off, I looked at myself in the mirror and almost didn't recognize myself. A faint knock on the door snapped me out of my trance.

"Hold on" I said.

"Jas it's me, open the door" Meka stated. I opened the door

nonchalantly like nothing had happened.

"Gee, you good?" she asked.

"Yeah, why you ask that?" I questioned as if I didn't know what happened.

"Gee, you just threw up all over people and shit."

"You sure? I know I spit up a little bit but that was in here" I retorted.

"Gee, you don't remember? You're drunk."

"Damn, I really don't remember. I feel fine. Let's go back out to the party." Meka looked at me funny, "You sure you're good? I think I need to take you back to my house" she advised.

"No, I'm good." I laughed, "What you need to do is let me go back out to this party" I sassed.

"Gee alright but let me know if you're ready to go" she stated surrendering.

"I got you."

I walked out without a care in the world, feeling myself until I was snapped out of my trance by some big ghetto girl screaming about puke in her hair.

"No, she gotta' go. She looks young, she shouldn't even be drinking. Like, damn. If she wasn't little, I would've beat her ass" she fumed.

I walked closer to see what was going on.

"There she goes right there. Put her ass out!" she demanded.

I watched where her fingers were pointed and looked behind me. No one was behind me. Looking confused, I stared at her for a few seconds until she abruptly shouted, "You, yes you lil' girl!"

"Bit--!" Before I could finish talking, Meka had my mouth covered and was pushing me towards the door. I tried to push Meka back towards the girl.

"No, don't try to shut me up. If she got something to say, she can say it to my face!" I exploded.

My struggle was to no avail. Meka held my shoulders and kept steering me to the door. By the time she finally let me go, we were outside on the porch. I snatched away from her and tried to push my way back in the house. Meka stepped in front of me and kept pushing me back,

"Calm down gee" Meka stated. She was bigger than me, so I was no match for her and the liquor in my system didn't help at all. I was so pissed; it didn't hit me until I calmed down that we were outside with no coats on in below zero weather.

"Jas, it's New Year's Eve and I don't wanna' ruin everyone's night by fighting. Just let that shit go. I mean, you gotta' understand where she's coming from. You and I both know if a bitch puked on you, the reaction would be the same way" she stated.

I tried to be serious but we both looked at each other and

laughed because it was true. In fact, my reaction probably would've been worse.

"Alright bitch, it's cold. Can we go back inside before we become one of these icicles hanging from the roof?" she asked.

"Shit, honestly this air feels good. I needed this fresh air" I admitted.

"Yeah, because yo' crazy ass drunk, and that liquor got you feeling all warm inside" she advised.

"Alright, I'll just go home. I don't feel like being bothered and I think I did enough at this party tonight."

"Alright, let's go get our coats and I'll tell them we're about to leave" Meka said.

"No, you don't have to leave. I'll just go back to the house I'm staying at" I announced.

"Jas, it's late. You know it's some crazy motherfuckers out here" Meka addressed.

"Don't worry about me" I said and walked back into the house. I grabbed jackets from the room and was headed for the door.

"Alright, be safe!"

"I'll be good!" I shouted back as I closed the door.

The late-night chill rushed through my body like a hail of bullets. I pulled my coat closed tighter and swiftly walked down the block to catch the bus. The more I walked, the more sluggish and drunk I started to feel. Walking faster and faster, I started getting paranoid. I finally reached the bus stop and sat down. I struggled to stay awake because I wanted so badly to fall asleep, exactly where I was seated.

The bus screeched to a halt in front of me and I rushed to get on. I held on to every pole trying to walk to my seat. The bus driver pulled off before I was seated which caused me to fall into a seat next an old man smelling like mothballs. What should've been a twenty-minute bus ride seemed like eternity as I struggled to stay awake. I knew I was drunk but sadly, I couldn't control myself. The entire ride, I fought to pull myself back up as I bounced and flopped every time the bus made any move. I could barely control my movements. The rest of the night was a blur, I'm not even sure how I made it in the house.

Wiping saliva off my face, I struggled to pick my head up. My head was throbbing, and I felt sick to my stomach. This is gone' be a long day, I thought. I felt around for my phone and found it pushed underneath the bed. I had two missed calls from my grandma.

Why was she calling me? I mumbled to myself.

I hit send to call her back and was greeted with her

screaming into the phone.

"Where you at girl?"

"Well, hello to you too grandma", I said in a sarcastic tone.

"Girl, don't get to starting with ya' smart ass mouth. Ya' momma said she was making you come back to Dallas. She said you're leaving in three days on Wednesday" she advised.

"I know, she called me last night. She's never strong enough to stand up to my dad. Why does she wanna' put me through all that abuse again? I'm starting to feel like she doesn't care about me" I sighed.

"Nah, you hush up with all that crazy talk. Yo' momma love you. She wants the best for you. But you're also her child, and she don't want nobody else raising you" my grandmother retorted.

"But grandma, you're her momma so I would be in good hands. Plus, a mother should want what's best for her child and being around that monster allowing me to get abused ain't what's best for me, or her!" I shrieked.

"Now lil girl, ya' momma want you home so you're going home. Don't think about running off and making me look for you because you will regret it! Make sure ya' ass get to my house sometime today so we can see you before you leave. Uncle Greg gone take you to the airport" she stated.

"Why do I have to come over there today?" I don't leave until

Wednesday and it's Sunday."

"Shit, you ain't my child I don't care what ya' ass do. Just make sure you here by Tuesday so Greg can pick ya' up and you'll stay with him and his wife that night."

I immediately hung up the phone, I didn't bother to acknowledge what she said. Before I could fully get off the floor where I was laying, my grandma was calling me again. I answered.

"Yes grandma?"

"Lil girl, I know you didn't just hang up on me. Don't make me come get you and snatch you up by ya' neck!" she screamed.

"Grandma, I didn't hang up on you. Okay, I'll see you later" I lied.

"Alright then, I ain't hear that but ya' better make sure I hear it next time" and the phone line went dead. I got up, pulled some clothes out my suitcase and got dressed. I didn't bother to even get in the shower. I shrugged; I could get in the shower later. But who was I kidding, I only opted not to get in the shower because I didn't want to be in that house any longer than I had to with Amber. If I had anywhere else to go, I would've left.

The past few days had been awkward. I was starting to feel unwanted. Amber was giving me the cold shower, every time I asked her anything or said something to her, she was responding with so much attitude. Nima wasn't around much and Angel had been giving me a stank face lately like she wasn't walking around here with her own problems, like her shit didn't stink.

Natasha had been questioning everywhere I was going lately, and I was becoming frustrated. Mostly everyone came and went as they pleased. I walked out of the house and walked down the block headed to Meka's house. I didn't feel like waiting for the bus. The entire walk, no bus had passed me anyway. I saw the bus coming in the distance so I stopped at the next bus stop. Once I hopped on the bus, I sat and stared in deep thought. I had a lot on my mind.

CHAPTER EIGHT

Uncertainty

Once I walked into Meka's house, I could hear Rico, a man that was like a father figure to kids in the hood.

"Good morning y'all. Happy New Year" I said as I walked in to meet everyone in the kitchen.

Meka was cooking pancakes for everyone. "Hey girl, when'd you get here? I'm glad you good because last night you were fucked up."

"I just got here, I told you last night I was okay" I stated.

"No, you ain't okay" Rico chimed in and said. "Come here, let me talk to you." I immediately got nervous because I didn't know what he knew. I walked up to him with my sweet innocent face on.

"Hey, Happy New Year" I said as I smiled.

"No, cut the act. What's wrong with you?" he questioned.

"Nothing's wrong with me. Why would you ask that?" I pretended to not know what he was talking about even though I figured he was referring to last night.

"Why were you acting like that at the party? You're getting so drunk that you're throwing up and on everybody's man" he addressed.

"I know. I'm sorry. I didn't know I would get that drunk." I felt embarrassed. I puked all over people at the party, now everyone would think I couldn't hold my liquor. Well, that was the reason, but everyone didn't need to know that. I wasn't a baby and I didn't like how he was trying to scold me like he was my father.

Rico was someone that was like a father figure, but he wasn't my real father, I didn't even listen to my real father. Rico was just a random nigga tryna' play daddy to the kids in the hood. Rico grabbed me and snapped me out of my trance.

"You listening to me?" he questioned.

"Yes, I am" I asserted.

"Be responsible. Don't let these nothing ass niggas take advantage of you. Get you a nigga that's gone' take care of you, that has some money and not on the corner tryna' hustle nickel and dime bags of weed. These dudes will wear the same pair of draws and jeans from three days ago" he continued.

Meka burst out laughing,

"You know we don't mess with bums. They can't even get a

reply from us" Meka bragged.

"You know we ain't lames and I ain't tryna' be stuck in a relationship with one of these lame niggas" I chimed in, smiling nervously. I hated being placed on the spotlight. Rico looked at me with an odd grin, *weird I thought.*

Meka continued talking but I tuned her out as I wondered why Rico kept staring at me, giving me a look as if he wanted to rip my clothes off at that moment. Usually I would be turned on, but coming from a grown ass man, I was grossed out.

"Hello?" Meka questioned as she snapped her fingers repeatedly in front of my face.

"Sorry, I didn't hear you. What did you say?" I asked.

"Were you daydreaming? Damn girl, I've called you about five times," she stated. "What you doing today? You tryna' hit the block today?" she asked. From the corner of my eye, I noticed Rico was still eyeing me up and down.

"Gee, I don't know. I just wanna' lay down. I don't feel good" I informed.

"What's wrong with you?" she asked.

"I woke up with a banging headache. I just feel overall sick and not in control of my body" I explained.

"You got a hangover" Auri stated laughing while running downstairs. "That's all that means."

"You want some Tylenol to help that?" Meka asked, chiming in.

"Yeah, give me something because I don't like this feeling."

Meka disappeared upstairs and brought back down two tablets.

"Here take these" she said.

"Y'all got some yogurt?"

"No, but we have some applesauce" she stated.

"Can you bring me some applesauce and a knife?" "What do you need a knife for gee?" she questioned.

"I need to chop the pills up and mix 'em into the applesauce."

"Gee, you're doing too much. Just swallow 'em" she insisted.

"No, they're too big" I explained.

"Too big?!" Meka asked shockingly. "You don't know how to swallow pills?"

"I know how to swallow pills; these are just too big" I retorted.

"Yo' 'wanna be' tough ass scared to swallow pills?" Meka questioned while laughing.

"Just try to swallow 'em, it's not that bad." Thirty minutes and three full glasses of water later, I was finally able to swallow the pills. I know I talk like I'm big and bad, but I'm scared to take medicine.

"Alright, I'm about to leave y'all" I stated.

"Where you going?" Meka questioned.

"My grandma called trippin' this morning saying I need to make it to her house today or she's coming to find me" I stated sarcastically as I rolled my eyes.

"You're in trouble?" Ziana asked as she walked in. "No, she just wants to talk to me, she's probably worried about me" I lied. I didn't want anyone to know that I would probably be going back to Dallas in the next few days. I didn't wanna' hear anyone's opinion. People were good with giving their opinions about situations that didn't concern them.

"What time did you need to be there?" Meka asked.

"There's no certain time, I just want to go early and let her see my face, so I'm not forced to stay there once it gets late" I explained.

"Yeah, come back because I'm tryna' hit the block and see what's poppin.'" Meka was excited to go to the block but I wasn't. I was focused on how I could persuade my mom to let me stay in Chicago.

"Meka walk me to the bus stop" I stated as I snapped out of my thoughts.

"You're gonna take the bus all the way out west?" Meka asked.

"Yeah, how else am I going to get there?" I asked sarcastically.

"How 'bout you ask Rico? You know dad ain't going to let

you take the bus all the way out there" Auri stated in a serious tone.

"Let you take the bus where?" Rico questioned as he walked into the kitchen.

"I need to meet my grandmother at her house. I was going to take the bus."

"Where does she live at?" he asked.

"She lives on the westside."

"Alright, I'll take you. What time you wanna' go?" he asked.

"I'm ready to go whenever y'all ready" I advised.

"You can come with me now, I'm gonna stop at my house for a while, then I'll take you" he stated.

"Okay, Meka, are you coming with us?" I asked.

"Yeah, I'll go with you. Let me get dressed" Meka replied.

"I wanna' go too!" Auri ran upstairs to get her coat.

We all piled in Rico's car and drove six blocks up to his place. While walking into the house, Rico casually held me back and told me we needed to talk. I noticed he waited until Meka and Auri were ahead of me and out of earshot before he stated we needed to talk.

Feeling nervous and uncomfortable, I twitched my fingers as I asked, "What do you want to talk about?" in a soft tone.

I was okay with talking since we were still outside in the driveway. I knew enough that it was better to talk in public, where there's witnesses and others could hear the conversation.

"I'll let you know once I'm ready to talk, okay?" he asked smiling as he put his arm around me and rubbed my shoulders reassuringly.

Alright" I stated as I slowly moved his arm from my shoulder, eyeing him suspiciously as I walked into the house.

Walking in, I slowly analyzed the place. The house didn't give off a 'home sweet home' vibe. If I didn't know any better, I would say it was a trap house. There was no furniture in the living room, just a dusty sheet hanging on the window being used as a curtain.

Stepping over shoes and dirty clothes everywhere, I made my way towards the back of the house. The first room I passed was similar to the living room. With a dark red sheet being used as a curtain and thin dirty mattress with no sheet, the room looked as if it was used to fuck random girls or run trains on them.

Bitches who let that happen were the bottom of the barrel; they had no respect for themselves. I know, I know, I'm a hypocrite since I had sex with a random guy, I'd only known a week. I still felt like it was more respectful than letting multiple niggas perform sexual intercourse at one time.

Walking through the house, the rooms looked the same except the last room. Meka and Auri were talking to Rico's biological daughter about going out to the rink tomorrow night. I wanted to go but I wasn't sure what would happen once I'd meet with my grandmother.

Rico's daughter, Ci-Ci, rubbed me the wrong way. I met her a year ago when I came back to Chicago for the summer. From the time I met her, she'd always stare at me. It seemed as if she was undressing me with her eyes and other times, she was searching my soul.

"Y'all could've waited for me gee. I didn't even know where I was going" I stated jokingly.

"You're so dramatic. I heard you and Rico talking so I kept walking" Meka stated laughing.

"Where's Rico anyway?" Auri chimed in.

"I'm not sure. He was still outside when I walked in." I felt Ci-Ci's eyes burning a hole through the back of my head as soon as I plopped down on the bed. Swiftly turning around, I caught her in the act. Annoyed, I rolled my eyes and turned around. "Y'all wanna' go out tonight?" I asked.

"Yeah, we can take you to your grandmother's house, wait 'til you're done and come back down here" Meka chimed in.

"Y'all can take me but I don't know how long she wants me to stay so I'll just meet you back down here."

"You can just call us when you're almost done, and we'll come get you" Ci-Ci stated.

"I'll hit yo' line if I need a ride. I might have a ride back over here through my cousin, Logan" I stated directly to Meka. I purposely ignored Ci-Ci because she annoyed me anytime she spoke, and I hated the way she looked at me. It was creepy.

"Gee, you gotta' make sure you can come back out tonight. I'm tryna' slide to Isaiah's house tonight. Gee please come with me" Meka stated.

"I don't play third wheel, girl no" I stated.

"You won't be by yourself. Isaiah said he got a homeboy that want you" she assured.

"The "homeboy" is usually ugly" I replied laughing.

"All his homeboys got money and they're older niggas. You said you needed a nigga' with money. I guarantee you'll get money from these niggas" she replied.

"I'm glad you know me. Money make me cum, not these niggas" I joked.

"True" Auri interrupted. "I need mon---."

"Girl, shut up. Yo' lil ass ain't getting money from niggas" Meka cut off Auri immediately.

"I do get money from niggas" Auri boasted.

"A boy gave me money to go to McDonald's after school" Auri explained.

"He gave you his lunch money?" Meka questioned sarcastically. Poor Auri went on for the next ten minutes trying to convince us she was getting more than five or ten dollars from her classmates. She had no chance. Meka had her share of finessing niggas and she wasn't impressed. I was too busy laughing to notice Ci-Ci had left the room.

"Auri you're still young. I can finesse some niggas too, I'll teach you" I reassured her. Rico appeared in the doorway to let me know he was ready to talk. He grabbed my hand, led the way to a room across the hall and closed the door behind us.

"Why did you close the door?" I questioned as I started to feel uncomfortable again.

"Just trying to give us some privacy" he replied smoothly. "I don't want everyone knowing your business, I wouldn't want to upset anyone."

"Why would they be upset?" I asked as I sat down on a stool close to the door. Rico pulled up a chair and sat directly in front of me.

Why so close? I thought. He was certainly too close for comfort.

"They're jealous of you" he simply stated.

"I don't think they're jealous of me. Meka has been like a sister to me for years, even Auri. Ci-Ci is cool with me, I believe." I included her because I figured it would be obvious, I didn't like her.

"They know you're pretty and have a nice petite shape. But let's get down to business. You're a pretty young lady and you're going places. You can get whatever you want from niggas' especially being a caramel skinned pretty young lady."

"Dark skinned girls are pretty too" I interrupted. I never understood why males preferred brighter skinned females. I felt dark skinned women were beautiful and often wished I had their complexion.

"I know they're alright too, but let's focus on you" he retorted. He was starting to annoy me. He seemed close-minded, but I was still curious to hear what he needed to talk about. "You said you needed money. right?"

"Yeah" I responded.

"You need someone that's gone' take care of you, right?" he asked.

"Yeah." By now, I was curious where this conversation was headed.

"I have somebody for you..." He took a short pause before continuing, "He's one of my friends."

Confused, I asked "What do you mean you have a friend for me?"

"His name is Meechie, he's a little older but he'll treat you good and take care of you."

"I'm not a prostitute" I blurted out. My entire face flushed, he looked at me concerned.

"Baby girl, you're okay? I'm not trying to upset you. Trust me, I would never hurt you. I'm not trying to pimp you. He's just interested in you because I told him you're a smart young girl, beautiful and need someone to take care of you."

Pausing to gather my thoughts, I considered what he was saying. Rico leaned in and caressed my hand. "I promise, I'm just trying to make sure you're taken care of baby girl."

"But I don't know this man. I need to see him, talk to 'em and make sure we vibe with each other before I start fucking with him" I huffed.

"That's easy. We can stop and meet him before I drop you off to your grandmother's house" He explained.

"Alright." He smiled at me reassuringly then left the room and disappeared down the hall, I followed behind and went back to meet the girls. I joined the girls as they were discussing hitting a party the "Get 'Em Boys" were hosting on the Northside this upcoming weekend. Of course, Ci-Ci's eyes were on me as soon as I re-entered the room.

"I can't wait to go!" Auri exclaimed.

"Auri you're not going. No one wants a little girl at their party" Meka interrupted.

"I'm not little and I bet these niggas' still gone' want me anyway" Auri exclaimed.

"I don't care. You're still not going with us!" Meka bellowed.

"Who is us?" Auri questioned.

"Jas, Ci-Ci and I, duh" Meka stated.

"I need a new outfit for this party. Their parties are always turnt" I chimed in. Meka agreed for us to go to the mall later that week. Lightly knocking on the door, Rico popped his head inside the room.

"Jas you're ready to go?" he asked.

"Yeah, let's go y'all." I gathered the girls as I got ready to walk to the car. Rico stepped into the room blocking the pathway to leave.

"How 'bout y'all stay here while I run her to her grandmother's house? It's not enough room for everybody to fit in the car with Ci-Ci going as well anyway." To my surprise, the girls quickly agreed to stay. I was a bit annoyed that Meka didn't try to protest knowing I had asked her to ride with me. I felt she should've gone anyway, especially since she had introduced us. Although he was like a father figure to some kids in the hood, my mom taught me not to trust these niggas; especially older ones who typically took an extra interest in teenage girls. But I was also getting desperate since my mom was sending me back to Dallas in a few days. I needed a plan.

"I'll be in the car" Rico stated as he headed to the car.

"Alright, I'll see y'all later." I chucked up the deuces and followed Rico. Once in the car, Rico started to give me a long seductive look from earlier when we were at Meka's house. I didn't know how to feel. Should I have felt grateful he cared so much or creeped out because he kept giving me long seductive looks? Every time he looked at me, he made me feel small like prey about to get pounced on. His eyes made him look creepy like a pedophile you would see on old television shows.

I tried to convince myself I was just trippin' and thinking too deep about it. After a long awkward drive that seemed like eternity, we pulled up to an older brownstone building on the Southside. The building had three floors. All the windows were boarded up except on the first floor. We got out and walked up the steps to the front door. Rico rang the doorbell while I followed at a distance, just in case I needed to run. Living in Chicago, you never knew what to expect. A tall dark figure appeared in the doorway.

"Wassup man" Rico stated as he greeted the unknown male by dapping him up, just as every black male greeted each other. I was dying to know who the unknown male was. I hoped it was Meechie because he was looking good. Standing about six feet tall, dark chocolate complexion that resembled black coffee, he looked like a stallion. His complexion reminded me of the R&B singer, Tyrese.

I eyed him, licking my lips. With a fresh pair of wheat Timberlands on his feet, True Religion jeans, an all-black hoodie on with his dreads hanging just below his ear he looked good enough to eat. He looked no older than 23, and I wanted him.

We all walked in the apartment on the 1st floor to the left

once we entered the building. Rico and Mr. Unknown walked down the hall towards the kitchen while I stayed in the front living room standing by the door. I was a little disappointed the unknown guy wasn't Meechie. I figured if he was Meechie then Rico would've introduced us when we walked in. I scanned the living room. It looked nice inside for a guy living on his own, I assumed.

I tried to fix myself up while they were gone. I hadn't seen Meechie yet, but this unknown guy already had my attention. There was a small mirror hanging on the wall next to the couch. I walked over and brushed up my hair with my hands. Hearing footsteps coming down the hall, I hurried back to the door and pretended to be fixing my nails. "Jas, this is Meechie. Meechie this is Jas" Rico stated. I couldn't contain my smile. Standing before me was none other than, Mr. Unknown.

"Hi" I uttered. I nervously tried not to make eye contact.

"How you doing?" he asked as he stuck his hand out to acknowledge me. I was immediately captured by his smile. He had a slight smirk on his face which allowed his dimples to show. Looking into his eyes, I got lost. Something about his eyes told a story. They were mysterious, seductive and dark.

"Damn, it's like that? No hand shake?" he asked chuckling.

"Oh sorry!" Snapping out of my trance, I quickly shook his hand.

Clearing his throat, Rico walked towards the door "I'll be back y'all, Ima' just run to the store to get a drink."

"Alright" Meechie replied. I knew that was only to give me and Meechie some alone time. Rico left out the front door and Meechie sparked up a conversation the typical hood way. "You smoke?" he asked.

Slightly chuckling, I replied "No."

"You mind if I smoke in front of you?"

"Yeah, you can smoke" I replied.

"So, you from 'round here, right?" he asked.

"Yeah."

"So, what made you move to Dallas anyway?" Taking a deep breath, I began to tell my story. I felt comfortable with him; the vibe was great with him. I didn't tell him about my hoe-ish antics, but I did tell him about my father, I told him what I wanted him to know.

An hour went by and we had learned quite a bit about each other. Meechie didn't have any children, he lived alone but visited his mother quite often in the week. He also told me his dad was killed a few years back, but it didn't affect him because he really didn't know him. I hadn't even noticed that Rico hadn't come back until he walked through the door and asked if I was ready to go.

Meechie stood up and gave me a tight hug. For some reason, I felt secure in his arms.

"Put my number in ya' phone" he demanded. Effortlessly pulling out my Obama' phone, I clicked the digits into the phone as he read them to me. Giving me a full smile with his cute dimples showing profoundly, he had me melting.

"Alright shorty, hit my line tonight" he remarked.

"Alright" I replied as I blushed. The ride to my grandmother's house was a lot less awkward. In fact, the twenty-minute ride seemed like five minutes. Pulling up to my grandmother's house, a lump filled my throat.

"You sure you don't want me to wait for you?" Rico questioned.

"No, I'm okay. I'll take the bus or find a ride if I decide to come back tonight."

"Alright, be safe" he stated.

"Thanks for the ride" I stated as I stepped out of the car. I waited until Rico left before walking up to the front door. I knew no one ever looked out the window but I didn't wanna' take any chances of anyone seeing him if I opened the door. Twisting the doorknob and pushing the door open, I immediately walked inside. I walked straight down the hall towards my grandmother's room.

I stopped in the kitchen to see what was cooked, my mouth watered. There was fried chicken, baked macaroni, collard greens, sweet potatoes and cornbread. I left the food alone and proceeded to my grandmother's room.

"Hey grandma" I stated as I walked into her room. She was laying down with a wet rag draped across her shoulders watching television.

"Hey Jasmine, I'm glad you're here. Come on in here and sit down" she stated in her thick Southern accent. Sitting down on her tiny bed, she immediately started nagging, "You can't stay here under my guardianship because I'm too busy and too old to be running after ya' fast ass."

"But grandma, I to---."

"Don't but me" she quickly cut me off. "Let me finish. You wanna' pull ya' cousin in your bullshit. Ashley is a good girl, don't try to pull her into yo' mannish ways. You forced her to stay out while you be fast with some lil' boys."

"Grandma I didn't force Ashley to stay with me. I ev---."

"No, I don't wanna' hear it."

"But grandma---."

"Hush! Whatever your dad is doing to you, it's not that bad. Yu can get through it. You need to be with your family."

With tears streaming down my face, chest heaving in and out, I was furious. I needed answers. My grandma left me sitting on the bed confused, hurt, and angry enough to want to punch somebody. I needed to talk to Ashley.

What did she say I did?

I desperately wanted to give her the benefit of the doubt and believe my grandmother was making her own assumptions. Something told me that wasn't the case. It was still early, I walked in the kitchen where my grandmother was on the phone chatting with one of her friends from church, as usual. I didn't bother to make myself a plate; I was no longer hungry.

"Grandma, I'm going to get all of my things from my friend's house, I'm coming back." Pulling the phone away from her face, she gave me a grimace look.

"You better come back! If I have to come looking for you, you gone' regret it. I ain't ya' momma and daddy. I ain't gone' play these games with you. Ya' hear me?"

"Yes" I replied.

Once I left the house, I dialed Miss Mary's number. The number was already saved in the phone my grandmother provided me.

"Hey Miss Mary, this is Jasmine."

"Hey, you're just the person I wanted to speak with."

"Oh," I chuckled.

"You have a few minutes to talk?" she asked.

"Yeah."

"Okay, I understand your dad is very mean to you and abusive sometimes. I also understand that it affects you more than you let it to be known."

With tears streaming down my face, I just listened. "But that doesn't give you an excuse or the right to run to Chicago and act a fool. Your mother still needs you. Did you think about how this would affect your mom?"

"Yes, I did but I'm a child and I'm supposed to be under her care. She chose to stay and allow both of us to continue and suffer the abuse, what about the well-being of her child? She doesn't care!" I exclaimed.

"Your mom does care about you. You chose to handle this situation incorrectly. Also, you're headed down the wrong path and you're trying to pull people down with you."

"Who did I try to pull down with me?" I asked confused and angry.

"Ashley told me you forced her to stay out with you while you entertained some boys and refused to take her home after she repeatedly asked." Without hesitation, I ended the call and blocked her from calling back. Finally reaching the bus stop, I sat down and watched traffic flow. Wanting to cry, I just slumped over and bit my nails. I was all cried out. Two busses and a train ride later I reached my destination. I was pissed Miss Mary knew all of my business. I wasn't sure who told her; but I was mad at everyone.

CHAPTER NINE

When You Least Expect It

Getting off of the bus down on Halsted, I pulled my jackets closed a little tighter. The sun had gone down, and the temperature had dropped. I walked swiftly a few blocks over to Amber's house. I barely knocked on the door before it was swiftly swung open. "Speak of the devil" Marcus stated sarcastically as he stepped aside to let me in the house.

"Bitch you a dirty hoe!" Amber shouted at me. Everyone was sitting around in the living room as if they were discussing me. I quickly scanned the room, the entire family, even BJ was there. I made eye contact with BJ, but he immediately put his head down.

"What the fuck? What are you talking about?" I asked.

"So, you gone' stand there and act like you ain't go and fuck Tyrek when I told you that I fuck with him?" she questioned.

"No, I didn't. I don't know where you got that from" I lied. Angel burst out laughing.

"You have the nerve to lie to my face? That's why yo' dumbass got exposed" Amber shouted.

"Who? What?" I stammered.

"Yeah, your dumbass was being recorded. I hope that lil' fuck and penis sucking you did was worth it" she sassed.

"Okay, you're mad about it and he don't even want yo' ass" I retorted. Looking over at BJ, I wanted to cry. My anger wouldn't let me drop a tear.

"No' I ain't mad, a hoe gone be a hoe" she shrugged.

"Bitch, I ain't no hoe! Ugly ass just mad you because you couldn't get a chance to fuck him if you tried" I provoked.

"Hold up, don't come in here tryna' talk shit because you got exposed. Amber is the reason you weren't homeless; you shouldn't have been out here thottin" Nima jumped up and stated.

"Bitch shut yo' fake ass up. You've came to me late at night talking shit about Angel and Amber. You even said Angel was lazy and ain't wanna' do anything but lay on her back." Angel was burning a hole through Nima head as she stared her down.

"That shit doesn't matter. We're family, we're always talking about each other, but you're not. You would fuck anything if they made you feel good for the moment. I'm sure it's other niggas" Amber calmly stated.

"Yo' lil' fast ass can't stay here anymore. I don't think you were being abused at home. I think you just wanted to do whatever you want and be fast in these streets" Amber's mom stated.

"I'm not a liar. I only came back to get my shit anyway" I retorted snidely.

"Bitch you better take that base out yo' voice talking to my mom" Angel snapped.

"Bitch worry about those kids you got running around here" I replied. From the corner of my eye, I saw Amber inching closer to me. She swiftly swung a left jab. I quickly ducked and followed with a right and left jab to her face. I'd had my share of fights growing up, so my reflexes were quick. I continued to swing as Amber fell into the television set. She managed to get ahold of my hair and held on for dear life. With one swift kick to the abdomen, Amber doubled over and loosened her grip on my hair.

I quickly pulled my head loose and stood up ready to pounce. Amber was left with two socks in her hand from the "sock bun" I had made and put in my head. "Bitch I'm going to kill you" Amber stated angrily.

"You gotta' get up to be able to do that" I retorted as I slammed my knee into her stomach and pinned her against the wall. Pain flared from my shoulder down to my back. I fell sprawled across the floor trying to cover my face as I was repeatedly hit blow after blow. I could tolerate the pain from the blows, but I didn't want my face to be scarred.

Angel had run up from behind me and hit me with a blow so fierce it sent me sliding across the floor. Before I could regain my stance, Nima pulled me by the hair as she sent blow after blow to my head. Frantically, trying to pull her down with me, I was met with Amber's shoe plunging into my side. With each kick, I got weaker. Feeling the need to vomit, I stopped fighting back and tried to cover myself.

This'll all be over soon, I thought.

I knew I had scratches and bruises because my face felt extremely hot. God please stop this. Let this be over soon, I silently prayed.

"Y'all ain't gone' keep fucking up my house. Just let her lil' 'fast' ass go. You can't change who a person is" Amber's mom stated. "Just let her up and let her go y'all" Keisha interjected for the first time tonight. Nima pushed me one last time then let me up. Amber disappeared into her room and came back out with my suitcase.

"Get yo' shit and get out" she spat as she flung my suitcase across the room, which landed at my feet. Picking up my suitcase, I left the house faster than I could blink. I just kept walking, I didn't know where to go or what to do. Finally stopping on 93rd and Cottage Grove, I laid my suitcase on the ground and plopped down on it. Tears began to flow uncontrollably. Feeling the need for comfort and a headache coming on, I decided to call Meechie.

"Who this?" a deep raspy voice answered.

"Is this Meechie?" I asked in a sweet innocent voice.

"Yeah, who is this?"

"Jas, the girl you met earlier with Rico."

"Aw, what's good shorty?"

"Nothing…bored" I went on.

"Aw yeah? I can keep you entertained" he stated chuckling. "Where you at?"

"On 93rd and Cottage Grove."

"You tryna' slide?" he asked.

"Yeah, I can but it'll take a while since I'm on the bus."

"Shorty I'm not gone' make you take the bus, I'll come pick you up" he prompted.

"Alright, but fair warning, I just got into a fight so I'm looking a mess right now" I stated nervously chuckling.

"Damn, you good? You 'bout that life huh?" he joked.

"Just some bullshit" I stated.

"Alright, I'm on my way. I'll be there in about twenty minutes" he advised.

"Alright" I stated. Feeling a little better, I watched traffic until a black care pulled up alongside the curb.

Who is this in this nice ass car? I thought.

A sleek, black Lexus with blacked out tinted windows and twenty-six-inch rims pulled up to the curb. I knew not to walk up to cars I didn't know so I didn't budge.

"Damn shorty, you gonna' get in the car?" I heard as the passenger window rolled down. Squinting my eyes, I leaned closer and realized it was Meechie.

He must be hustling to afford this car, I thought.

Smiling, I started tugging my suitcase towards the car.

"I got it. Give me your suitcase, go get in the car" he stated. Meechie got out of the car, grabbed the suitcase, then opened the passenger for me to slide in.

"Thank you" I replied. I watched as he put the suitcase in the trunk, I examined the car.

He has some good taste.

I rummaged through the car to see what I could find before he got back in. Hearing the trunk slam, I began scrolling through my phone pretending as if I was busy.

What am I doing? I thought. *No one would want to show off this cheap ass phone,* I said to myself.

We pulled off, headed down 87th towards the low-end on the Southside, blasting Future's song "Rich Sex." As we passed the expressway, he lowered the music. "So, are you gone' tell me what happened?" he asked. Taking a deep breath, I began telling my story. "I was staying with my friend who I grew up with."

"So yo' ten-year home girl, huh?" he questioned smiling.

"Yeah, I guess you can say that" I replied. "We started bumping heads since we've been living together, and I overheard her talking shit about me with her other home girl. She ended up constantly trying to make me look bad in front of her brother's friend because she liked him, but he liked me."

"Damn, that's crazy" he interjected. "Yeah, so I hadn't been there too often the past few days but today I went to pick up the rest of my shit to go to my grandmother's house for a while, but we ended up fighting and her family jumped me."

"Them bitches just jealous of you, you're a cute ass lil' girl" he stated.

"I'm not a lil girl" I stated as I rolled my eyes.

"Oh yeah?" he questioned as he chuckled.

"Do I look like a lil' girl to you?" I questioned with attitude.

"My bad shorty, I ain't mean to offend you" he smirked as he raised his hands as if he were surrendering.

"You're okay" I stated, laughing nervously.

"Don't worry about all of that though. You're still cute."

"Thank you."

"You're welcome" he replied. "I assume you don't plan on going back."

"No, I don't."

"You got another place to stay?" he questioned.

"Not really, I could go to my grandmother's house but I'm not tryna' go there. It's too many people living in that house" I stated.

"Yeah, I understand that. My mom's got a house full of people too. You can stay at my crib tonight, if needed, I ain't trippin" he responded.

"I don't wanna' bother you. I'll figure out somewhere to go by tonight" I stated.

"Shorty, you ain't no bother. I definitely don't want you out in the streets by yo' self. These streets ain't nobody friend" he replied.

"True, I guess I'll stay for the night" I sighed.

"Alright, you hungry?" he asked.

"A little bit."

"Alright, you want some Harold's chicken?" he asked.

"Yeah."

"Alright, bet" he affirmed.

Five minutes later we pulled up to Harold's chicken shack. "What can I get y'all?" a short caramel skinned girl asked at the front counter in a thick accent. Being away from Chicago so long, I now realized we did have an accent.

"Get whatever you want" Meechie stated. He didn't have to tell me twice, I loved when niggas said those lovely words.

"Can I get a three-piece chicken wing combo fried hard with extra mild sauce and a Wildwood Cream soda?"

"Anything else?" the cashier questioned.

"Give me the same thing she's having and that's it" Meechie stated. We ate at the restaurant instead of taking the food "to go" and shared some laughs. Meechie was a cool person. He seemed like a laid-back guy until you pissed him off. I certainly didn't take his kindness for weakness. He seemed like he had another side to him, one that I didn't want to know about. Leaving the restaurant at about eight o'clock pm, it was completely dark. It felt so much later in the day. I hated daylight savings time.

We pulled up to Meechie's crib a few minutes later. I followed closely behind him as he walked up the stoop to unlock the door. He even let me walk in before him. Most niggas would walk in before you and expect you to follow. Once inside, he led the way down the hallway to his bedroom. His bedroom was nice. A sleek, black leather bedroom set, he even had a headboard.

Most niggas I fucked with had their beds sitting on crates or on stacked up yellow pages. They only owned the mattress and box spring, having a headboard was foreign in the hood. I was impressed. I stood awkwardly as he fished in his drawers for a t-shirt and basketball shorts to sleep in.

"I can sleep on the couch and you can sleep in here tonight" he stated as he handed me the clothes.

"Can I take a shower?" I asked.

"Yeah, the towels are down the hall in the closet across from the bathroom" he replied.

"Thank you, I'm gone' go get myself together then" I stated shyly.

"Alright, I'll be in the living room if you need me."

I walked down the hall slowly as I was trying to look at the pictures on his wall and see if I recognized anyone. Once I reached the bathroom, I wasn't surprised or disappointed. I expected his bathroom looked exquisite since the rest of the house looked that way as well.

Decorated black and coral, it looked as if a female had decorated it. I shrugged it off and turned on the water to run my shower. While pulling my clothes off, I caught a glimpse of myself in the mirror and was horrified. I had dried up blood along with scratches all over my face. Seeing myself, I wanted to fight all over again.

I can't believe those bitches jumped me.

I wanted revenge. I knew I would eventually catch them all one by one sooner than later.

After thirty minutes in the shower, I felt rejuvenated and refreshed. I dried myself off and put on Meechie's oversized t-shirt and basketball shorts. His shorts were falling which caused me to roll them up three times. I walked out and heard Meechie on the phone. He noticed me and told the unknown person he would hit them later. I wanted to ask who he was on the phone with, but I knew it wasn't my place.

"Feeling better?" he asked.

"Yeah, you could've told me my face was fucked up like this" I stressed.

"You're still beautiful either way" he smirked.

"If you say so" I simply replied. He stared at me in silence and I became nervous. I wasn't scared, I just felt like soon I would be riding his penis all night. It had crossed my mind, but I wasn't ready for that.

"Umm, these shorts are too big. Do you have some smaller shorts?"

"My bad shorty, those are the smallest I have" he replied.

"It's okay, I'll deal with it."

"Alright, you wanna' watch TV?" he asked.

"Yeah, what movie or show you got in mind?" I asked.

"Let's find something on Netflix" he replied.

Giving him the side eye, I became annoyed. "You're not about to get the perks that come with "Netflix and chill" I stated snidely.

"Chill shorty, I ain't that type of guy. We can even sit on separate couches." After giving him a long stare, I finally agreed. He got comfortable on the shorter couch while I laid sprawled across the longer couch. For the next few hours, we watched movies until I began to doze off. After smoking a blunt, Meechie began to doze off as well. Unable to fight sleep any longer, I went back into Meechie's room and got comfortable.

I couldn't bare sleeping in Meechie's big ass shorts, so I closed the door, took off the shorts and got into his king size bed with nothing but his t-shirt and my panties on. Once I began dozing off, a slight knock began on the door. "Come in" I stated. Meechie slightly opened the door and peeped his head in.

"Shorty, you alright?" he asked.

"Yeah, I'm alright. I'm about to go to sleep" I advised.

"Alright, you want me to close the door?" he asked.

"Yeah, thank you and good night."

"Same to you" he responded. I plugged my phone up and seen I had 15 missed calls from my grandmother, four from my mother, and two private calls. I forgot I had placed the phone on vibrate, but I didn't want to talk to any of them, so it was perfect. I turned the phone off and placed it on the charger for the night.

CHAPTER TEN

A New Day

I woke up feeling relaxed. *I haven't been this relaxed since I originally left Chicago,* I thought. I turned on my phone then got out of bed and went straight to the bathroom. I stayed in the bathroom for a few minutes only because it felt comfortable and safe to me. I almost didn't want to leave. I hollered out of the bathroom asking Meechie if he had any spare or extra toothbrushes.

"Look in the cabinet on the first shelf" he stated. I found the spare toothbrushes and picked my favorite color, purple. After brushing my teeth and washing my face, I walked out the bathroom and ran into Meechie coming down the hall. He seemed to be taken off guard and kept staring at me, at my body. I immediately apologized when I remembered I only had on a t-shirt and panties.

"It's cool shorty. I see you needed to get comfortable, but I'm cool with that" he replied. I swiftly walked past him and hurried into the bedroom. "There's some McDonald's in the microwave I picked it up earlier this morning if you're hungry" he hollered down the hall.

"Okay, thank you" I replied. Once I put on some shorts, I retrieved my food from the microwave and retreated into the room.

"Aye shorty, I gotta' go take care of some business but if you need anything, hit my line" Meechie stated.

"Alright, do you know how long you'll be gone?" I asked.

"Shit, about four hours" he advised.

"Okay" I replied.

I watched as he walked out of the house in some True Religion jeans, wheat Tims, and a white tee with a grey hoodie pulled over his head. He looked so good. By the way he was dressed, I knew he was about to hit the streets to get money. He was a hustla' and it was evident by the way he dressed and carried himself. He wasn't a nigga you wanted to play with or cross.

Since Meechie wasn't expected to be back for a few hours, I decided to take another shower. After double-checking the door was locked, I grabbed the dry towel Meechie had given me last night from the room and headed towards the bathroom. Once showered, I fished out some leggings and a t-shirt.

A soft buzzing sound filled the room, my mother was calling. I watched the phone ring and vigorously shake until it went to voicemail. I wasn't ready to talk to anyone. I was still mad, honestly, I was pissed! A notification for a text message came,

'Where are you? I have all of your flight information, call me.' I slammed the phone shut and tossed it on the nightstand. That was one of the many perks of still having a flip phone. I eased back into the bed and turned on Netflix. Meechie's bed was super comfortable.

I had been in plenty of beds, but this was by far, the most comfortable bed I'd ever been in, especially for a man. I plopped down on the bed, grabbed the remote, and turned the television on. I turned to one of my favorite crime television shows, *Law & Order: SVU*. They were having a marathon, so I got comfortable and tuned in. Not long after, I was nodding off to sleep. Hearing a sound as if loud bricks were hitting the floor, I panicked. Jumping up, I ran out of the room ready to attack and see what the commotion was. I followed the noise to the kitchen and found Meechie slamming two fists full of grocery bags on the table.

"Oh, it's just you" I stated relieved as I walked in.

"My bad, I didn't mean to wake you up" he replied as he kept putting away groceries.

"It's okay." I leaned against the wall and watched him walk back and forth putting away groceries. He was handsome. I snapped out of my trance and walked back to the room before he became suspicious. I checked my phone and was not surprised of the amount of notifications. I had six missed calls from my grandmother, three missed calls and three texts from my mother. All three messages asked, *'Where are you?'*

I slammed the phone closed and placed it back on the nightstand. Just as I placed the phone down, Meechie appeared in the doorway with no shirt on and a lit blunt in his hand. I almost fainted.

Damn, I wanna' be on top of him, I thought to myself.

He waived his hand in front of my face. "Hello?" he questioned.

"Huh?" I replied.

"Damn, shorty, you can't hear me?" he asked.

"Oh, so- sorry, what did you say?" I stuttered.

"I asked if you wanted something to eat" he replied smirking.

"Yeah."

"Alright, I'm ordering pizza" he stated.

"Okay" I replied.

"Shorty, you ain't gotta' stay locked in this room, you can come in the living room. I ain't gone' bite" he proclaimed.

"I don't wanna' bother you, I didn't wanna' invade your personal space" I replied softly.

"Come and watch a movie with me" he stated.

"It's about to snow anyway so we 'bout to be in for the night." I followed him into the living room and plopped on the couch. "It's cold out here" I whined. I could hear the wind slapping against the window causing it to shake. After handing me a small blanket from the linen closet, Meechie handed me the remote to pick a movie while he called to order pizza. I got comfortable on the couch and picked a low budget hood movie that I heard was good.

Truthfully, low budget hood movies didn't receive enough credit. They directly portrayed what was going down in the hood that people not from there didn't see or care about. Meechie sat back down on the couch extremely close to me. He was so close that his cologne was intoxicating me, and his skin rubbed against mine.

Although I was uncomfortable, I didn't ask him to move because I wanted to feel him. Shit, I wanted to feel him inside of me. After readjusting to a more comfortable position, he began watching the movie while I watched him. His penis print was poking through his jeans and it looked like a monster. I was feenin' for some lovin', not just any lovin', but some good lovin.' Five minutes into the movie, Meechie placed his arm around me. He thought I was oblivious, but I was fully aware.

Since he wants to play this game, Ima' play right along with him, I thought as I chuckled to myself.

I leaned in closer and began resting on his chest. He looked at me and I smiled. "What?" I asked in an innocent voice. Time went by and we began to get into the movie. It was a good movie; I would've noticed before if I was paying attention. The doorbell rang just in time. I didn't know how much longer I could hold out before I gave up and ended up sucking his manhood while his finger was in my ass.

Meechie went to the door to get the pizza while I attempted to pull myself together. He came back with paper plates, napkins, and two Wildwood can pops. "How many slices you want?" I held up two fingers.

"Oh, so you can't talk now?" he joked.

"I just felt like doing that" I chuckled. We made "small talk" while eating then immediately went back to being snuggled up together on the couch. We didn't even bother cleaning up our mess. Meechie began rubbing my lower back as I laid on his chest. I snuggled closer to let him know I was comfortable and wrapped my arm around him as if we were hugging.

As I laid on top of his chest, I felt his heartbeat increasing as well as mines. If I could feel it, I knew he felt the same. I felt his hands inch lower and lower down my back until he reached my ass. His hands palmed my ass in a firm grip. I loved it! I looked up and met his eyes, I blushed. He leaned down and kissed me then gazed into my eyes. He slipped his tongue in my mouth and our tongues intertwined. We explored each other's mouth as he laid me down on the couch. He tugged on my shorts and I lifted my ass while he slid them off. He slipped his fingers in between my thighs and made his way to my sweet center. He looked at me shockingly and looked at my juices all over his fingers. "Damn, you wet as hell shorty."

"That's because I'm ready for you to be inside of me" I stated softly as I gave him my puppy dog eyes.

"Oh yeah?" he asked.

"Yeah."

He gave me a mischievous grin and proceeded to lick all of my juices from his fingers. I was ready. He bent down, stuck two fingers in, and massaged my pussy while he sucked and licked all over my titties. He took his time with me. I was in heaven. He began kissing every inch of my body then sucked on my pussy like a pacifier. He lifted me up and carried me to the bedroom and laid me down gently all while sucking on my lips. He walked to the dresser to retrieve a condom then pulled his fat juicy penis out. My mouth watered, I immediately hopped up and assumed the position. He had eaten my pussy so good that I wanted to return the favor.

I had great balance, so I didn't bother to get on my knees. I squatted down on the tip of my toes and slid his penis in my mouth. I slid two fingers in and out of my pussy while I slid his penis in and out of my mouth. I sucked him so good, I had him moanin'. I was feeling like that bitch! Even with my jaws locking and damn near choking myself, I kept going. I knew he was loving it because I looked up while I sucked him off and was pleased with the image I saw.

His eyes closed, mouth wide open, with a firm grip on my head, he was feeling good. "Ooh, ooh shit...I'm, I, I'm 'bout to cum" he stuttered.

"Then give me my nut baby" I paused and stated. I gave him that 'sloppy head.' "I'm cummin.' I kept sucking and he filled my mouth with cream. I happily swallowed and kept going.

"Damn shorty, you a beast. You tryna' make a nigga' fall in love." He stepped back, picked me up, carried me to the bedroom, and laid me on the bed. I was ready to feel him inside of me. He kissed me sloppily as he slid his fingers in and out of my sweetness. He slid out of his pants and slid my shirt up over my head. We were completely skin to skin. Meechie moved closer to me and I felt his penis dangling between his legs. He bent down, palmed my face and swirled his tongue in my mouth as we kissed like it was our last night together. Meechie began a trail of sloppy wet kisses from my neck, down my stomach, to my legs. I closed my eyes in ecstasy and savored the moment. I gasped for air as Meechie slid his tongue in between my toes. The feeling was sensational; he had me ready to have his baby.

He kissed me, slipped on a condom and slowly slid himself inside of me. Gasping, I immediately tensed up. He continued to push himself inside of me. He was so big. "Relax baby" he whispered as he continued to stroke himself in, I allowed him more and more access. The pain began to turn into pleasure. He had me in ecstasy. By the end of the night, he had flipped me, tossed me, and folded me up like a pretzel. He arched my back so much while giving me back shots, he had my back throbbing. He bent me over onto the dresser and forced me to look into the mirror while he stroked me from behind. He looked at me through the mirror and smirked while he watched me moan in ecstasy until we climaxed together.

Meechie had me feeling like a virgin again. After pleasing

every inch of my body, we laid together fully exposed. He held me from behind with his manhood pressed into my ass. He kissed my neck and pulled me closer. I felt safe and secure in his arms.

I closed my eyes and said a silent prayer asking God to keep him in my life and allow him to continue to take care of me. I thanked him for bringing him into my life. I know he hadn't been in my life long, but he had shown much more care for me than any other man had ever done in my life. He was heaven sent.

In two days, he had managed to make me feel precious instead of like damaged goods. We laid together with our legs intertwined and fell asleep for the rest of the night. The next morning, I was awakened to the smell of buttery pancakes and eggs. I opened my eyes only to realize I was alone. I threw on Meechie's t-shirt that was laid on the dresser and went to locate the source of the lovely smell.

Meechie was in the kitchen scrambling eggs in a pan.

He cooks? God, you're just showing out with him now, he's everything!

I stood back and observed him. Nothing was sexier than a man willing to get down in the kitchen. I admired his body. He was standing with grey sweatpants on and no t-shirt.

"Good morning" I stated. He turned around looking scrumptious.

"Good morning big head" he stated as he smiled. "You hungry?"

"Yes" I replied.

"Sit down, I'm almost done" he stated. I sat down at the kitchen table and watched as he made my plate. He handed me my plate and watched me as I ate.

"Stop watching me" I whined.

"You're beautiful. I just wanna' admire that" he stated. I blushed as I continued to eat. After eating, we walked back to the room and Meechie put my body into overdrive. After sex, my pussy almost felt as if it was crying. Meechie twirled his tongue up and down, in and out, and around my clit. He was so sweet; he massaged my clit after he pounded me like no other. We both climaxed together.

Meechie slipped on his clothes to leave while I laid in the bed and got comfortable. "Aye shorty, I know it's been a few days since you've been here, and I've been seeing you ignoring ya' family calls. I'm not kicking you out, you can stay here. I'm enjoying ya' company and I'll help you get back on ya' feet and get this money. Trust me, I got you" he stated.

"I don't wanna' overstep my boundaries. You're used to living alone" I stated.

"I've lived with females before and I don't want you to leave. Matter of fact, I'm not letting you leave" he stated while smiling. Blushing, I looked away.

"I'll think about it", I stated.

"Alright shorty, I'll be back in a few hours. I gotta' handle some business" he stated. I knew that meant he was about to get some money.

"Alright" I said. After kissing me and walking out, I heard the front door slam a few seconds later. I fished out my phone from the nightstand and was greeted with 68 missed calls from my mother and 21 messages. I didn't bother reading the messages or returning the phone call. I sent a quick text to my mother.

'Hey mom, I love you and I pray that you gain the courage to leave like I did. My father is toxic, and I don't deserve to be beaten and verbally abused, neither do you. I'm not coming back to live in a toxic environment. I will not be coming back. I love you and hope I get to see you again one day. Don't bother looking for me because you'll be unable to find me. I'm safe, I love you.'

I sent the text and turned off the phone. I figured I no longer needed the phone. I didn't need anyone but Meechie. I buried the phone deep in Meechie's nightstand and hoped to never have to bring it out. I decided I would stay with Meechie. I laid down, snuggled up with the blankets and watched television while I waited for Meechie to get home.

CHAPTER ELEVEN

Betrayal

Hearing keys jingling in the door, I jumped in excitement. I missed Meechie. He had been gone so long that I'd watched about five episodes of Grey's Anatomy. It was only three in the afternoon, but I missed him. I met Meechie just as he was opening the door. "Wassup shorty? What you up to?" he questioned as he walked in a greeted me with a juicy kiss on the lips. I didn't even allow him to close the door before attacking him with kisses. I grabbed his face and sucked on his bottom lip. It felt good to be able to suck on his lips.. I savored his lips and after a while allowed him to savor mines. I wanted him.

With our tongues intertwined; Meechie pushed the door close with his hand and struggled to lock the door while we kissed. Meechie then picked me up and carried me to the couch. He laid me down and proceeded to undo his pants. I quickly grabbed his face and pulled him down closer to me. I craved his lips, his scent. I craved him. Our tongues danced together as I helped him slide his pants down. I briefly paused and allowed him to do away with his clothes. While he removed his pants, I removed my shorts and tank top. I pulled his body down towards mine. I wanted to feel him. I wanted skin to skin contact.

"You missed me baby?" Meechie questioned as he licked up and down my torso and played with my belly button. "Yes; you know we missed you daddy" I moaned.

"Who is we?" He asked as he dipped his tongue into my honey pot.

"Me and —yo—yo pussy; you know it's yours" I stammered. I could barely get the words out because Meechie's tongue felt like ecstasy.

"I like the sound of that" he chuckled. Meechie licked, sucked, and slurped on my clit until I came on his face. He lifted his head and smiled at me. I bent down and tasted my juices on his lips. I loved when he kissed me after dipping in my cookie center. They were my own juices, so I didn't care.

I slipped my tongue in and out of his mouth as I slowly pushed him back into the couch until we had switched positions and I was on top. I left a trail of succulent kisses on his chest until I met with his joystick. It was time for me to play. I licked the tip then allowed his full joystick inside to come and play. "Gimme' my nut daddy" I uttered. "I'm about to cum" he panted. I sucked harder and got ready for him to release his kids but Meechie didn't allow it. Meechie pulled back and shot his kids all over my face. Jumping back; I immediately began scrubbing my face looking over at him wide-eyed.

"What?" He questioned shrugging.

"I wasn't expecting you to do that" I whispered.

"Oh, now you mad? See you ain't no freak like you try to make it seem" he criticized.

"I'm not mad; I actually liked it" I stammered rushing to give him a kiss. If it was anyone else, I would've been furious and considered it disrespectful. But Meechie was like no other; he was teaching, showing, and introducing me to new things. I was grateful. "Well show me you like it then" he smirked. I climbed on top of him, grabbed his manhood, sat down on it and rode him like no tomorrow. Meechie worked me over so well; he gave me an experience I'd never forget.

"You're hungry?" he asked as we laid sprawled across the couch trying to regain some energy.

"Yeah; I could eat" I decided.

"You like steak?" He asked.

"I love steak" I happily replied. I loved that he loved to feed me.

"Let's go eat at Ruth's Chris Steakhouse downtown. Get dressed" he insisted as he texted someone on his phone.

"I've heard of that restaurant, but I've never been there; isn't that a classy restaurant? I don't have clothes to wear to that type of establishment."

Alright don't worry about that shorty; we'll get you some clothes on the way there" he offered.

"Alright, can I get in the shower first?" I asked.

"Yeah; hurry up though" he contended. I quickly grabbed a towel and ran in the bathroom. I was excited. I had always wanted a nigga to take me on a date to Ruth's Chris. I heard it was a nice upscale restaurant that cost a pretty penny. I didn't mind him spending that on me. I was in and out of the shower and dressed in twenty minutes. It didn't take me long since I didn't have many clothes to choose from. I slipped on some sleek blue jeans, an all-white fitted t-shirt and my cocoa brown boots with fur lining the top. I still wanted to look presentable just in case he changed his mind about getting me some clothes.

"I'm ready" I stated as I walked into the living room to meet Meechie. He had gotten dressed while I was in the shower. Meechie sported some fresh wheat Tims, all black True Religion jeans, a white tee, an all-black pull over hoodie over and an all-black beanie hat. He looked True Religion and Tims. He looked damn good! He could have on nothing but a wrinkled t- shirt with holes and he would still look good to me. By now it was about a quarter to six pm. We left the house, got in the car, and headed to dinner. The closer we got to downtown the more I felt accustomed to wearing the outfit I had on. I was a little disappointed he wasn't getting me a new outfit since I didn't have much clothes anyway. I had come to Chicago with only one small suitcase of clothes and shoes. I could barely get through the week without re-wearing a previous outfit. That was the downfall to running away. You had to pack light.

About twenty minutes later we pulled up on Michigan Ave and parked. Meechie paid the meter then we walked about two blocks down and entered in the Water Tower. I became a bit anxious and excited. I didn't wanna show too much excitement and make him think I wasn't used to this. The Water Tower is a huge indoor shopping mall in downtown Chicago. Mostly people with money shopped here. Back in the day me and my homegirls would come here during their busy times and clean them out. We were so good, we would take everything from clothes, shoes, to hair accessories. They had over a hundred stores with seven floors; it was easy to steal and disappear into the crowd. I had never actually bought anything out of the mall. Everything was free for me and my homegirls from around the way.

We rode the escalator up to the third floor and walked towards Akira. "Go pick out whatever you want or need, and I'll wait out here; I gotta make a phone call. Come let me know when you finished" he ordered.

"Okay" I stated nonchalantly.

Inside I was filled with excitement, but I didn't wanna let him know that. I walked into Akira and went crazy. It was so many things I wanted but I didn't know what type of spending he was allowing me to do. I picked out an off the shoulders oversized tan sweater and an all-black pair of pants that resembled 'wet paint.' I finished the outfit with some tan combat boots along with some matching pearls to go around my neck and a set of silver earrings. I was in love with diamonds and pearls. I couldn't wait 'til I got some real money and bought my first pair of real diamonds and pearls. I wanted that 'rich white lady drinking bottomless mimosas at brunch with my crew' type of money.

I took my items to the front register. "Hi ma'am, you ready to check out?" the clerk probed popping her bubblegum loudly. "Not yet, one second" I remarked as I walked out the front door of the store to find Meechie. He spotted me before I could get to him and immediately hung up the phone.

"You ready?" he asked as he walked towards me.

"Yeah" I replied. Meechie followed me back into the store.

"I'm gone get you thick" Meechie stated as he smacked me on the ass while once, we got to the front register. "Stop" I whined as I playfully pushed him. The lady rang up my items and the total came out to $86.53.

"You only got one outfit and some jewelry; whatever that shit is you got up there. You want something else?" he asked.

"I do need clothes, but I don't' wanna spend all your money" I stated sadly. I was hoping my emotions were getting to him and he would buy me more clothes. It wasn't all bad. I did wanna spend his money, but I had a good reason; I really needed clothes.

"Shorty stop playing with me. I already told you to get whatever you need and want. Now hurry up!" he stated in a serious voice. I immediately picked up three pairs of blue jeans, one light colored pair, a black pair, and some dark blue jeans. I grabbed five solid colored t-shirts. They were easy to pair with almost anything you had on. I picked up another pair of combat boots; all-black in a size seven and sat down and tried them on. They fit so I also picked up three different pairs of leggings in colors I could wear any day or time. I chose navy blue, black, and grey. I especially loved grey leggings, they made me look thicker. Who didn't love that?

I walked back up to the register and piled the clothes on the counter. Meechie was already there waiting for me. The cashier rang the items up. "Your total is $217.56 she stated. Meechie pulled out a wad of money rolled up and counted out $220. After paying for the items, we walked out, and **Meechie** sent me to the bathroom in the food court while he sat down. "Go hurry up and change" he stated in a low sexy voice.

I rushed to the bathroom, changed my clothes and fixed my hair. I threw my old clothes in one of the shopping bags. I checked myself out in the mirror before walking out. I looked good. I met **Meechie** back in the food court at a table. "How I look?" I asked as I walked towards the table.

"You look decent shorty. Now let's go" he stated as he looked me up and down. He grabbed my bags from me, and we exited the mall and ended up back on Michigan Ave. I squealed inside that he was treating me this way. He carried my bags for me, and he was spending his coins on me. We walked over to Dearborn Ave and went inside Ruth's Chris steakhouse. I was a little uncomfortable with Meechie carrying all of my bags and we were in such a nice restaurant. I thought we were going to stop by the car and load the bags in the trunk, but Meechie had other plans. "Table for two?" The greeter asked.

"Yeah" Meechie replied.

"Would you like a table or a booth?" She asked perkily.

"A booth" Meechie answered.

"Right this way" the greeter stated as she led the way to a booth in the back corner of the restaurant next to a window. "You guys enjoy. The waiter will be right with you" the greeter stated as we sat down, and she handed us our menus. I didn't look at the menu long, it was a steakhouse, so I always got a standard meal. "What you want shorty?" Meechie asked.

"I want a ribeye steak, well done, with asparagus and loaded mashed potatoes with no chives" I replied.

"Damn, you know how to eat" he stated chuckling. Once the waitress came, Meechie ordered the exact same thing for both of us along with red wine for himself and a Sprite for me. The waitress brought our drinks and we made small talk while we waited for our food. I watched Meechie sip the wine and I wondered what it tasted like. I kept having flashbacks to the night of New Year's Eve. I definitely didn't wanna' feel like that again. I paid the price for it the next morning. My head was killing me. "You want some?" He asked. He noticed me watching him.

"No, I was remembering the night I had on New Year's Eve with alcohol and I didn't like the feeling" I stated.

"Wine is different from alcohol. Just try it; you'll like it" He urged.

I took a sip of his glass and I liked it. It was smooth. You could barely taste the alcohol; it was almost like juice.

"Can I have the rest?" I asked as I took another sip.

"Yeah, I told you you'll like that shit" he laughed. Once our food came, Meechie ordered two more glasses of wine. He took a few sips from one then handed both to me. I happily took the drinks and gulped down both glasses. I really liked the red wine. Meechie finished all of his food while I could only finish half. Meechie summoned the waitress and asked for the check. "Would you like a to-go box ma'am?" she asked.

"Yes ma'am" I replied. She brought a to-go box back, loaded my food in the container, and loaded it in the bag. She handed Meechie the bill and waited for the payment. Meechie sat the bill down and pulled out a wad of cash. I glanced at the bill and couldn't believe my eyes. It was $193.46, and Meechie didn't even bat an eye when he saw it. In just a few hours he had spent a little over $400 and it was spent on me. Meechie gave the waitress $225 and told her to keep the change. We didn't stay to get the receipt. Meechie grabbed my bags and led the way out the door. We headed back down Dearborn street and crossed over back onto Michigan Ave.

Meechie piled the bags in the car while I stood back beaming. I felt as if I was floating. I could tell I was starting to get buzzed. I loved the feeling.

Meechie and I hopped in and we sped down the Dan Ryan expressway back towards the hood to his house. Once we got back to his house, Meechie grabbed a "burner" phone out of his top drawer in his room that could easily be disposed. He was headed right back out the door. He had a drawer full of prepaid phones with prepaid phone cards that you could easily activate. It was odd to me; I still didn't know what Meechie did for a living, but I knew it was illegal. I didn't bother to ask; I figured he would tell me when he was ready. I figured the less I knew the better.

"I'll be back shorty; hit my line if you need something" he stated as he walked out the door. I undressed, hopped in the shower, slid on a big t-shirt and panties. I got in the bed and waited until Meechie came back home.

Over the next few weeks, Meechie treated me like a queen. Meechie found out I didn't know how to drive and began teaching me. I became a pro at driving. I asked Meechie if I could drive the car to the corner store one day by myself, but he refused. He said he needed to protect me when I was out since Chicago could be crazy at times. Just last week a female was shot in the head a few blocks from where Meechie stayed for sitting in her boyfriend's car. It was a case of mistaken identity. I wanted to be independent, but I understood his reasoning. He would only let me drive the car when he was in the car with me. I was a little bummed he didn't let me drive by myself, but I didn't wanna seem ungrateful. He had done a lot for me.

He bought me the brand-new iPhone that had recently came out with one condition I didn't give the phone number to anyone. He said since I had run away; the phone number could be tracked, and the police would come take me and him. I didn't want that to happen so I promised no one would have the phone number. The only person who called and texted me was Meechie. I was happy to have a phone, but I was bored since I wasn't talking to anyone else. I checked my Facebook periodically, but I never posted or spoke to anyone on there. Besides Meechie teaching me to drive and buying me a phone, he had been spoiling me tremendously.

Two months had passed and Meechie had taken me on four shopping sprees to build my wardrobe. I was loving it. Besides occasional shopping and Meechie loving on me nonstop; I stayed holed up in the apartment most of the day. Although I loved Meechie pampering and treating me like a queen; I missed going to school. I had everything I wanted but I wanted to be around my homegirls. I hadn't spoken to them since Rico had dropped me off at Meechie's place.

Today was no different, I was laid up in the bed waiting for Meechie to come home. We had been sexing like porn stars, whenever he was home and all throughout the house. Meechie walked in and I happily greeted him at the door. "Hey baby" I stated as I kissed him.

"Wassup shorty" he stated as he picked me up and carried me to the bedroom and laid me down in the bed.

"Let's watch a movie and cuddle" I suggested as I watched him get out of his clothes.

"Baby not tonight, I got company coming over" he stated.

"I wanna' have a calm and intimate night with you, please" I pouted.

"I can't cancel this business I gotta' handle baby, but I promise we gone have our alone time tomorrow night."

"Alright" I sighed disappointed.

Meechie grabbed a towel out of the closet and got in the shower. Once he was out the shower, he began catering to me. It was normal for us to engage in intercourse almost every night, but tonight was different. Meechie took his time with me. Meechie grabbed the baby oil off the dresser and massaged and caressed my body. Once he finished, he briefly left the room and brought back a glass of red wine almost filled to the brim. "Here baby, relax" he stated handing me the glass.

I sat up and downed the drink quickly because I wanted to get back to him caressing me. He took the glass, refilled it, and told me to drink up. I downed the second glass then laid back down across the bed.

Meechie left a trail of kisses starting from my neck down to my toes. A chill went down my spine as he licked in between my toes. Meechie moved back up and began savoring my pussy. I couldn't help but to watch Meechie, I couldn't believe the feeling he was giving me. I was on cloud nine. My vision began getting fuzzy. I was feeling the full effects of the wine. Meechie put himself inside of me, I felt as if I was high. By the time we finished, I had orgasmed three times and Meechie had left my legs shaking uncontrollably. I wanted more but Meechie wanted me to save my energy for later.

Afterwards I felt faint, I didn't bother putting on clothes. I laid sprawled across the bed while Meechie left the room to make a phone call. A few minutes passed and Meechie came back in the room to let me know his friend was coming over for a while. The room felt as if it was spinning, I didn't respond. I heard voices in the living room, so I knew his company had arrived. I tried blinking and rubbing my eyes to focus but it didn't help. Meechie appeared in the doorway along with his friend. I tried to jump and cover up, but I barely moved, I didn't feel in control of my body. "I'm naked Meechie, get him out of here" I stammered.

"Relax baby, my homeboy wanna' taste some of you too baby. You want me to continue taking care of you then you need to help me" he stated. I wanted to get up and leave but I could barely move. I didn't feel drunk anymore, almost like stuck in a trance.

I watched hazily as Meechie left the room and the tall dark figure walked in. He began touching me and I flinched. He stepped out of his clothes and slipped on a condom. I wanted this to be over, but I felt stuck. I closed my eyes and allowed him to have his way with me. Once he finished, I felt him rip the condom off and he had the audacity to leave it laid across my stomach. I just laid and cried. I desperately wanted to get up, cover up, and leave but I couldn't. I heard laughter coming from outside the room.

Meechie walked in a few minutes later and kissed me on the forehead. "Good job baby, it was yo' first time so I know you're scared but you'll get used to it" he stated.

Meechie left me alone in the room for the rest of the night. I woke up the following morning feeling different. I felt Meechie hadgiven me more than just wine, but I couldn't prove it at the time. I slipped on some clothes and walked out of the room to realize Meechie was already gone.

I took the opportunity to leave. I grabbed my suitcase out of the closet and stuffed all the clothes in the suitcase. I searched the room up and down for the phone Meechie had bought me, but it was missing. I gave up and went to obtain the old government phone I had originally came with, but it was also missing. The entire drawer with the "burner phones" and prepaid phone cards were gone. I began to get angry. I opted to just leave and find a way to contact Meka once I left.

I went to leave out the front door, but the knob was missing. It had been replaced by a deadbolt on the inside! I had never seen anything like it. I went to the window in the living room to climb out, but I quickly discovered all of the windows in the entire apartment had bars on them. I ran around the apartment for almost an hour looking for a way out but was unsuccessful. I quickly realized I was trapped. I knew I was stuck. I sadly walked back into the room, put my suitcase back in the closet, crawled back into bed, and cried myself to sleep.

Over the next few weeks, I quickly realized Meechie didn't care about me. To him, I was easy income. The bedroom that I thought was once ours had become a revolving door of different men paying to have their way with me. I was disgusted. One night I pleaded with him to let me go; he refused. I told him Meka and Rico were like my family and they trusted him. I begged him to allow me to call him. I soon found out I was set up.

"Bitch, nobody cares about a hoe. Why do you think they sent you to me? Meka alerted Rico that you were good for the job. I met you and knew ya' naïve ass would fall for me; I groomed you and got you ready for this life. Bitch you owe me!" he shouted.

Meechie began beating me if I refused or gave the men a hard time. I tried screaming but in the mist of him beating me I found out the entire apartment was soundproof. I still replayed the words he said over in my head, "Bitch nobody can hear you, it's soundproof. Now shut up before I beat yo' ass again. Nobody cares about yo' ass anyway" he stated.

I was extremely hurt. I found out Meechie had been slipping me Percocet's and Xannies in the wine he was giving to relax me and keep me high. Most of the time I was out of my mind but being sober caused all the feelings to rush back to me and I wanted to kill myself. I was forced to continue taking the pills to not think about it. I desperately missed my mom. I didn't even know what day it was. I began altering between Percocet's and Xanax pills to get through my days. The weeks soon turned into months. I had been locked inside the apartment going on five months. I could tell it was around summertime because Meechie no longer used the heat and the apartment was warm most days.

Each day I scratched a tally into the bedroom floor since I had spent so much time there. Most days I sat in the room looking out the window wondering if anyone was looking for me. After over a hundred failed escape attempts, I had no hope. I was going to die here. I kept thinking of what my grandmother would tell me to do. I could only think of one thing, so I dropped down on my knees and prayed.

CHAPTER TWELVE

Revenge

The next day I woke up and completed my daily routine, that is until Meechie started bringing my "clients." He called them my clients and told me to think of my body as a business. He would constantly tell me I should be happy I was making money and that the customers loved my "business." I was nothing but a dollar sign to him. It was his business and I was just an employee. I worked for him while he reaped the benefits. Some would even call it slavery. I never seen any of the money. Meechie paid me in Percs and Xannies while the clients handed the dough directly to him.

Each morning, Meechie had a Perc and a fresh bottle of water waiting on the dresser for me. I showered, threw on some all-white shorts that barely covered my ass and a matching white bra. Meechie kept me in check by making sure I never had on many clothes. He said less clothing was advertisement and it served no purpose by being covered up. He also kept me that way to ensure I wasn't hiding anything. He would even do random sweeps between clients. Lately however, they weren't so random; he was getting sloppy. I noticed he came to do a sweep in the room after every two clients and I began to expect it.

I popped the Perc, took a swig of water, went to the window and began my morning routine of staring and thinking until my first client came in the corner of the room by the window

Out of the corner of my eye, I spotted a gum wrapper in the bottom right corner of the window, stuck to the outside, with writing on it. It was a small white gum wrapper with small handwriting. I squinted and bent closer to make out the words. The window was dusty and extra thick due to being soundproof so it was a bit difficult. The words *"Jas dis Meka, you safe?"* were scribbled across the wrapper. I slammed my fist into the window and screamed out in pain. The window was high from the ground and Meka was fairly short.

How did she reach the window? I thought.

I fell back against the bed. Meechie bust in the door ready to pounce on me. "The fuck is yo problem?" He asked. I quickly straightened up and explained I tripped and accidently hit the window.

Meechie stared at me for a moment "pay attention next time dumbass" he grimaced. He walked out of the room, slamming the door. I was in pain but more enraged by the message.

How could Meka leave that message when she was the reason I was here?! I was furious, she knew I wasn't safe!

Why would she try to reach out to me? I thought. I didn't even know if it was truly her. The small writing said Jas but she usually called me Bubbles. I recalled Meechie telling me Meka had told Rico I was a good fit for Meechie and basically selling me to him. The message put me on edge, my curiosity grew. *Was Meechie lying* I wondered or was Meka trying to antagonize me? I decided to try to get a message back to Meka to see what would happen.

After all, what's the worst that could happen? I thought.

Meechie would beat me like he always did, I was starting to wear my scars proudly. If no one else cared, why should I? A nigga would do that to you. He would break you down so much, you would even start believing the shit he said about you.

My first client for the day was a middle-aged guy named Richard who went by Rich. In the months he had been coming he'd been the nicest to me. I always hoped he would help me get outta' here one day but so far the day hadn't come. I snuck an old Harold's receipt out of his back pocket while getting him out of his pants and proceeding to punish him by spanking him with his own belt. Rich liked kinky. I fished the receipt out balled it up like trash until I had time alone. I moved quickly because I felt the perc taking over my body. I threw it onto the floor in the corner because I knew Meechie wouldn't notice. Meechie mostly did sweeps to check for extra tips and/or little gifts like jewelry some of the clients would give me.

Once I finished with Rich I watched Meechie leave the brownstone, and went to work on finding a pen or pencil to write with. I knew Meechie would be gone a while because I overheard him screaming at someone about not taking over his territory over on Essex.

Meechie had lil' corner boys who hustled weed in the hood. Some upcoming hustla named, Dee, was tryna' come for his spot and he wasn't having it. They had been trippin' the past few weeks, they were playing tit for tat, hitting each other stash houses or robbing each other's corner boys. I found an old red pen and scribbled a message *'Not safe, need help.'* I fished a bottle of Honey out of the kitchen cabinet and dabbed some on the tip of the receipt and ripped the remaining paper off to make it as small as possible. I stuck the receipt to the bottom corner of the window and fanned it until it stuck.

The next few days dragged, I checked the window daily and there was no sign of Meka, I didn't even know if she had seen the note. Hell, I didn't even know if the note was from her. After three days, I peeled the old receipt off the window and gave up. I was stupid to even think she would come help. After all, she helped sell me to Meechie.

I had been seeing less of Meechie since he had been getting a lot of heat in the streets from Dee. I was secretly happy Dee was applying pressure to Meechie. I wanted Meechie to take a loss and I didn't care how. He deserved it. Although I was happy about his possible downfall, I was panicking and craving for him to get home and give me my daily dose of Percocet's. Since he had been on the move lately I had no clients and because I was locked inside since he didn't wanna risk me escaping and that meant no payment, no Percs, and no food for me. I felt panic creeping over me as I experienced cold sweats and a racing heart, not to mention the increased cramping and nausea I was having. I found myself not eating and barely sleeping.

After a lost count of days that had passed, Meechie finally busted through the front door with three of his homeboys right behind him. I didn't know their names, but I had seen em' around a few times. They were amped.

"Get the Glock and load all that shit in the car" Meechie barked as he stuffed one duffle bag with money. I watched one of the guys punch the code into the safe and remove two Glocks. Meechie never let me close enough to get the code when he went into the safe.

"Bitch you stink" Meechie growled pushing past me as he went into the room and changed his clothes.

I leaned against the wall for support while watching Meechie move around the room frantically. I was sure to stay out of his way. He changed into some black sweats, an all-black hoodie, a black skull cap and some all black air forces. They were all dressed in all black. Whatever they were up to they meant business. It was the type of look that said "I'm about to put that nigga in a body bag."

Meechie was fuming. I stood off to the side watching, making sure not to get into his way. I didn't want him taking his anger out on me.

Just as one of the guys opened the door to head to the car, Meka stood in the doorway. "Damn Meka, where you been?" one of Meechie's guys asked. Meka was pushed inside of the apartment by a tall light skinned dude with dreads. Five guys entered the apartment toting AK 47's.

Shots rang out everywhere. Although I hated life, I didn't wanna die before I had fully lived. I tried to run for cover, but a bullet ricocheted off the refrigerator and hit me in the left side of my abdomen. I doubled over and dropped to the ground. A burning sensation overcame me as if I was burning from the inside out.

"*Arghhh!*" I cried out in agony. The rain of bullets soon came to an end and I noticed Meechie and his homeboys sprawled across the floor with bullets in them. Meka was face down on the floor with one of the unknown guys holding a Glock against the back of her skull. There were tears rolling down her cheeks. Meka starred at me with defeat in her eyes. She hadn't been shot yet but the guy holding the Glock to her head looked eager to put a bullet in her skull.

We weren't leaving the house alive.

Blinking rapidly to avoid tears, I desperately thought of ways to prolong my life. I didn't wanna' die. The tall guy with dreads trotted over to me with his heavy Timberland boots.

Who wears Tims in the summer? I thought.

As he got closer, my eyes began playing tricks on me. If I

make it out of this, I never wanna' experience this again. The guy was starting to look like my first love, Deon. The guy who took my innocence.

"Deon?" I croaked.

"Damn girl, I done tore this whole city up for you" he proclaimed as he chuckled.

"Deon, it's you!" I shrilled.

"Yeah it's me" he confirmed as he bent down to pick me up. How did you find me? I questioned. I grunted as he moved me.

"Yo Dee, we gotta go bro" one of the guys interjected as he peered out the window. The sounds of sirens in the distance growing closer.

"Dee? You're the one Meechie been tripping with in the streets?" I asked in pain.

"Yeah" Deon responded.

He lifted me and carried me to the car. All the guys followed except one. Another gunshot rang out and I knew Meka was dead. Inside I cringed because I'd loved her, we were once friends, but she deserved it. She sold her own friend. "We gotta get you patched up" he stated. I know a doctor, I'll have 'em meet us at one of my spots" Deon stated. Deon sat in the backseat with me while another sat in the passenger and two more guys hopped in another car parked along the street, a Dodge Charger.

The last guy ran out of the building, hopped in the driver's seat and we sped down the block headed to Deon's spot. The Dodge Charger followed us. I leaned against Deon for support in the back seat of the car as he applied pressure to my wound. I was getting weak.

"After you left the state, I had everybody call me Dee", he expressed. "One of my guys went to Meechie about some business one day and he recognized you, snuck a picture of you and brought it to me. I kept tabs on you and later found out he was pimping and beating you. The guys know I don't play about you and never did. I couldn't risk him knowing I was coming to get you, so I started hitting all his spots to make him think I was tryna take over his territory. My guy told me Meechie was fishing for another girl and about to pawn you off to some old pimp on the North side, so I had to act fast before that happened. That snake ass bitch Meka would be on lookout for him to make sure you never got out or nobody ever came towards the door, so I had to snatch the bitch up for the plan to work" he stated as I tried to listen. I began coughing up blood and Meechie pushed down harder on my wound.

"Hold on shorty, we almost there" he consoled as he left the doctor, he had on speed dial, a voice message.

"I left that note on the window hoping you'd figure out a way to respond. I didn't put my own name because I didn't want you thinking it was a setup by Meechie.

"Damn, I'm glad I left a note for you" I replied.

175

"Yeah, I'm glad you did too" he stated.

"I had been following the nigga all day and he led me right back to you. Jas, I had to come get you. I don't break promises. "My love don't have an expiration date. No matter how long or how far, I'll always come back for you" he professed.

My heart melted. That was the same thing he would always tell me since 8th grade. He remembered.

As we raced down the back alleys, I listened to Deon apologize over and over "I'm sorry you got shot in the process" he stated solemnly.

"I'm just glad you came for me I stated, I can live with a gunshot wound" I croaked.

For the first time in years, since being with Meechie, and living with my father, I felt love. Not just any love and certainly not that conditional love I got from Meechie and my dad. Not that type of love that came with conditions and stipulations. It was unconditional love. I knew I was safe; it wasn't just a feeling.

Made in the USA
Middletown, DE
13 September 2021